Money & Blood

by
Wayne Dean-Richards

Illustrations by
Tony Chenery

with an introduction by
Paul McDonald

'...money ... people are rich or poor, make a living or don't have to, are useful to systems or superfluous. And blood—the way people live as families...'

—Grace Paley

Acknowledgements

Versions of the stories have appeared in the following publications:
'Almost'—Rumble Fish Press (US); 'Driving Instructor Number #1' —Wild
Pressed Books Pamphlet Series; 'Clock-Radio'—*Runcible Spoon*; 'Roofer'—
Cry of the Poor (Culture Matters, 2021/23); 'Opportunity'—*The Raconteur
Review*; 'Why I Did What I Did to My Dentist'—*Lumpen*; 'Today Next Year'—
One Hundred Voices anthology (US); 'Yard For Rent'—*Flash Fiction North*.

Introduction

By Paul McDonald

In my years teaching creative writing at the University of Wolverhampton, the guest writer I'd ask back most often was Wayne Dean-Richards. There are several reasons for this: a teacher himself, Wayne could speak fluently about his aesthetic, his writing strategies, and his influences; he was clearly someone who thought deeply about writing.

More importantly, the students liked his accessible, regionally based stories of working-class life: many were from a similar background, knew Wayne's fictional terrain, and felt the authenticity of his account. I was convinced they would learn worthwhile lessons from studying his lean, scrupulously managed prose: the value of significant detail, economy, subtlety, irony, and understated humour. I hoped too they'd learn to value the familiar and domestic as a source of material in their own creative lives. At a time when *Harry Potter* dominated undergraduate reading, it was useful to remind them that baristas, driving instructors, hairdressers, salesmen, and shop assistants have as much dramatic potential as wizards.

I've been reading Wayne's writing for well over thirty years. When his stories began to appear in the little magazines of the late 80s/early 90s, I'd seek them out, recommend them to friends, and study his style. They'd often appear in journals that rejected my own work, and for good reason: from his early days as a writer Wayne's fiction had a patina of sophistication that mine lacked. He wrote the kind of stories that I longed to write, but couldn't: a seemingly effortless, Carveresque minimalism that seethed with controlled tension.

The late 20th Century was a rich time for West Midlands fiction writers, and some who emerged in those years, like Jonathan Coe and Jim Crace, achieved international acclaim, but life can be tough for those who favour short stories, and it's fair to say that Wayne hasn't had the recognition he deserves. Though widely published in magazines, with several short collections to his name, this is his most substantial collection to date, and it's a joy to see it.

The consequences of capitalism: hierarchy, exclusion and alienation

Anyone familiar with Wayne's work will recognise the themes in **Money & Blood**, chief among them being, as the title suggests, money and blood. The corrupting power of capitalism and its tragic, often violent consequences can be seen throughout the book. In 'Wasteland', for instance, Palmer's moral decline is examined against a backdrop of consumerist desire, from Ted Baker suits to luxury 4x4s. Very often such moral decline is borne of the pressure to succeed, one which bears particularly heavily on male characters: many, like Palmer, are acutely status-aware, and struggle with inherited definitions of masculinity.

The materialist mindset develops early for the kids in 'Spiderman #2', where the narrator realises that his little brother is right to privilege price over value: when violence erupts over the devaluing of a comic, it offers a clear life-lesson about our market-driven world, underscoring the link between money and blood. Male competitiveness sometimes takes on absurd comic dimensions in these stories, as in the 'one-upmanship' clash between Tom and Freddie in 'Lads', and we frequently see men face emasculating failure, overcompensating in the gym, the pub, or via misogyny and violence.

Naturally this affects the women in their lives: when David in 'Driving Instructor #1' finds his status as 'top instructor' threatened, for instance, his wife is forced to start shopping at Ann Summers; when the eponymous heroine of 'Vicky' pushes a local gangster into a canal, she must face him in a boxing ring in order to appease her challenge to masculine power.

Sometimes Wayne's heroes seek forms of redemption: occasionally this is ironic, as with Josh in 'Reward Points', who finds a novel way to compensate his ex-wife for his shortcomings, but more often it is darkly obsessive, as with Hanson in 'Seaside Towns' whose search for his absent father is driven partly by resentment, partly by psychosis: we can only guess at the connection between the former and the latter.

Elsewhere the legacy of abuse is darker still: it's revenge rather than redemption that motivates the hero of 'Notes from an Angry Young Man', for instance, who directs his own 'great anger' at society after a lifetime of mistreatment by his alcoholic dad. Such lives are shaped mostly by the past, and an inherited ideology: inherited values, inherited financial constraints, inherited systems of hierarchy and exclusion.

Wayne Dean-Richards may not be an overtly political writer, but it's hard not to think in political terms when we read his work. The inequities of capitalism, and the values and assumptions that accompany it, frequently underpin the conflicts that drive his fiction. Alienation, alcoholism, broken relationships, diminished self-worth, and mental illness pervade these stories, and the connections between money and blood are everywhere to be seen. Wayne has been writing such stories all his life, and few would argue that they feel more relevant now than ever.

Contents

Vicky

Unseen by the stern—looking dinner lady, I'd climbed the railings at the top of the school field. On George Road, turned hard left and crossed the sloping car park of Dr Crawford's surgery to the tall trees bordering it. The muscles in my arms and legs trembling with the effort climbed to the top of the tallest tree and was looking down on everything when Mr Proud drove onto the surgery car park in his S type Jag and got out.

"What's this about Vicky Hopkins?" he demanded.

It was about the fact that in classrooms I felt suffocated and up here I didn't. Though because I knew Proudy'd turn purple if I said so I shrugged.

"Don't you shrug at me young lady," he snapped.

It seemed—four months shy of my tenth birthday—I wasn't a girl anymore. And probably explained why he rang my old man and told him if my behaviour didn't improve, I'd never amount to anything.

For a long time, I thought he was right, though when I first worked at TREVOR'S I barely had time to think at all.

Parked at the edge of the industrial estate off Cakemore Road and every few minutes rocked by the clatter of trains slowing into or accelerating out of the nearby station his fast-food van had done so well Trevor Kennedy decided to expand.

Looking me up and down he said, "I suppose you're a great cook?" Wanted someone to work in the old TREVOR'S while he worked in a new one five miles away. He who'd hand-painted his name onto their sides. In both cases the serving hatch directly under the V.

Expecting to be rejected as a result I shook my head.

"Good, I don't want somebody who takes half an hour to make a bacon butty." He said I mustn't allow a queue to form—though Office Supplies, Key Services, and Tyres & Exhausts had their breaks and lunches at the same time —then handed me a blue and white striped apron.

I liked that it was a one-woman show. No one looking over my shoulder or ordering me about. Things good until the day Trevor Kennedy pitched up, said, "I've got to let you go," and pointed.

Office Supplies and Key Services had shut down and Tyres & Exhausts looked as if its days were numbered—a man in oily overalls sitting on a lopsided deckchair out front reading a newspaper.

Walking along the canal towpath with my hands stuffed into my pockets I saw a family of ducklings and reeds bowed by the wind. Wished sunlight would glint off gold coins instead of an abandoned pushchair. In my mind saw them exploded across the silted bottom. Knew the water was bitterly cold and stank of rot but wouldn't hesitate. Lying face down on the flagstones would grab those gold coins up off the bottom as if my life depended on it! When I had it wouldn't matter that Trevor Kennedy had given me my marching orders! I'd be able to buy a little house, with a garden. A swing in it for Izzy and a tall tree in it for me.

But seeing no treasure found myself remembering a dream in which a horse's head bobbed just beneath the surface. The panic of this dream what distracted me. Why I didn't notice what was going on under the bridge until I was practically on top of the two men.

My mother was even thinner than me. Told me she'd always been a worrier. Worried sick whenever she had nothing to worry about. Worried she might put something in the dustbin the bin men would refuse to take she wrapped everything she chucked away in old newspapers. Wore baggy trousers and oversized woollen pullovers that flapped as she worried herself from one job to another.

On the day she died, we'd been to the pictures. An afternoon showing because I worked evenings at the Amber Tavern. I don't remember what we saw, just that her eyes were bloodshot. Put it down to her wrapping her old newspapers in old newspaper and suchlike. Knew if I mentioned it, it'd only make things worse.

We walked rather than spend money on bus fares and not for the first time she told me the story of her life through the films she'd seen. The Reel and its earlier incarnations where she'd seen each of the Bond films as they came out. Connery her favourite. Why growing up whenever one of his was on telly, we watched it together.

Our trip was my birthday present to her, and she thanked me. "That's alright," I said and hugged her. But quickly. Was meeting Carl for pizza and had to be at the Amber Tavern for six.

It was busy when the hospital rang. The after-work crowd in. The jukebox so loud I almost didn't hear my phone.

When I hung up, I told the boss I had to go. Intended to tell him why until he said, "If you go, don't bother to come back." Would he have back-tracked if I'd told him my mother had been rushed into hospital with a sus-pected heart attack? I didn't put it to the test, said, "Fuck you," and stormed out.

Blinded by headlights from the Hagley Road I called Carl three times, but he didn't pick up.

When the taxi dropped me off at the hospital, I have no idea if I followed signs, thumbed elevator buttons, hurried along white-walled corridors. All I know is my mother died before I got there.

The one wearing a blue denim jacket was getting the worst of it. The other man—jacketless—shoved him against the wall and hit him in the face, hard.

I ran towards them. The smack of my trainers on the flagstones like applause. The bridge was one I'd walked under many times. How I knew at head height KEITH OF WEBSTER MOULDINGS IS A BASTARD was sprayed onto the crumbling brickwork and the middle of the three flagstones was cracked.

Bleeding from the nose Denim Jacket tried to kick Jacketless and missed. The force of his kick throwing him forwards and bringing him to his knees.

Before Denim Jacket could scramble to his feet, Jacketless was on him again. How I had the time to lower my centre of gravity. flatten my palms and drive my hands into the middle of his back.

Caught by surprise Jacketless pitched forwards—across the cracked middle flagstone and headfirst into the canal.

Would he drown? Shocked by what I'd done I was relieved to see him surface, but not to see him scramble to pull himself out. He had short blonde hair. An eagle tattooed to the side of his neck. It was clear he wanted to kill me and still I didn't move until he said, "Stay there, cunt!"

Denim Jacket ran from the under the canal bridge. Turned hard right and sprinted up an uneven blue-brick path to reach Rounds Green Road.

When he glanced to his left, he saw me alongside him.

We ran to the end of Rounds Green Road and descended a grassy bank onto Sainsbury's car park—out of sight of the road.

Denim Jacket bent at the waist and put his hands on his knees. Had a Keanu Reeves thing going on with his hair.

I was gathering myself to go when he straightened up and said, "Shit, Vicky, you shoved Will Stepney into the fucking canal." Laughed and said, "Stepney's Ronnie Smith's man!"

"She's had a great day," Mandy Mizlocki said. Ran Tots out of a three-storey Victorian house Izzy liked to pretend the two of us lived in. Had a kid the same age as Izzie and smiled a lot though her teeth were as crooked as mine. Always said something about the kind of day Izzie'd had though I couldn't help wondering if today she told me her day had been great because she saw it was what I needed to hear. My suspicions further roused when she asked me if I was OK.

"Things have been hectic," I admitted.

The sound of a tantrum exploded behind her. "See you tomorrow," she said. Hurried away as I took Izzie's hand in mine.

Holding her hand helped ease the anger some of the recent quiet spell at TREVOR'S had let surface.

My anger directed not at Carl for fucking Jaslin Sahota when he was supposed to have been watching football with his friend George Douglas, but at me.

Despite an earlier warning, I hadn't put two and two together until Carl came home geared, put his arm around me and said, "Jaslin, babe."

Even then, I might have let him squirm away if he hadn't tried to cover his mistake by saying, "I don't know anybody named Jaslin, honest!"

My warning had arrived a week before Izzy was born.

Carl was in a good mood that day. Said the match he watched with George the night before was, "Full of passion," and started sprinting along the aisle. Was going so fast he almost drove the trolley into an old man reaching for a tin of tomato soup.

"Watch where you're going," he snapped. Had played centre-back for the school and—never inclined to undersell himself—told me if I wanted to imagine him in his playing days I should think of, "John Terry at his best."

Alongside a loaf of the cheapest Aldi bread, the old man had two tins of beans in his basket.

"Are you fucking deaf?" Carl snapped.

I said, "Carl? Let me introduce you to my dad."

Ten minutes later Carl was happy to give us father-daughter time while he hoisted our shopping into the boot of his battered Fiesta.

As if he were contagious, I kept a good six feet away from my old man.

He said, "When's it due?"

I said, "What do you care?"

Might have eased up on him if he hadn't glanced over at Carl and—though it looked as if it pained him—said, "I don't think he's to be trusted."

Convinced my old man had left us for another woman I said, "You'd know all about that!"

Izzy said, "I like parrots." We were nearly home. She had on a sky-blue dress. Had put her own hair in bunches. The parrot in the stories Mandy read them could talk and Izzy wanted to know if all parrots could. I told her I thought so. Happy to hear it, she grinned and was content to walk in silence until she said, "When will I see dad again?"

The one-time Carl came to the house he wasn't quite pinging off the walls, though his eyes kept shifting as if he was looking for something just out of sight.

He said, "I'll bring some money next time I come."

I didn't ask if he was working. Didn't see how he could be if he was still coming down during an afternoon visit.

"We're fine," I said, though we were barely scraping by.

He'd lost weight. Had two razor nicks on his left cheek. "I'm not with Jaslin anymore," he whispered.

Izzy sat at the table. Her legs scissoring back and forth. Had on an orange-coloured dress—Satsuma what I'd been calling her until Carl's unannounced arrival—and was eating cheesy potato and salad whilst pretending not to but watching Carl and me closely.

"Just in case you were wondering," Carl said.

I took a single cup from the drying rack. "You said you'd take Izzy to the park."

Carl turned to her. The first time he'd looked directly at her since he arrived. He said, "Next time, OK?"

That was six months ago. When would she see him again? "I don't know," I said. Wanted to say something that'd comfort her, but as we turned onto Edmunds Road saw Lee the Landlord's Audi.

The first time I met Danny Lee he said, "Call me Danny." But I never had. From day one thought of him as Lee-the-Landlord. A man who wore a sheepskin jacket and made his living renting damp-splotched old houses him and his brother had divided up into apartments.

We rented the ground floor of 39 Edmunds Road and Lee-the-Landlord always stopped by a week before the rent was due.

My stomach churned. How would I be able to keep from my face that as of today I was jobless and practically broke?

Izzy said, "Can we have fish fingers for tea?"

I said, "We'll have to pop to the Co-Op to get some."

She nodded to show willing as Lee-the-Landlord got out of his Audi and knocked at the front door. When no one answered, he'd push a photocopied slip of paper through the letterbox. At the top it said: RENT DUE NEXT WEEK. Underneath it said: DANNY LEE—LANDLORD. I'd always wanted to cross out DANNY LEE—LANDLORD. Replace it with LEE-THE-LANDLORD and tape it to the front door before his next visit.

"Can you run?" I asked Izzy.

"If we can sing," she said.

We sang as we ran.

The keyboard was missing a couple of keys and the internet was slow. Not that if the keyboard had been perfect and the internet was like lightning it would've made any difference—there just weren't many jobs where you could earn enough to live on.

When I pushed back my chair and stood up two men made a beeline for the computer I'd logged out of.

The one who reached it first put his hand on it as—two steps off the pace—the other made his way back to Bleakhouse Library's few remaining large print westerns.

Hearing, "Vicky Hopkins," I stepped over to the desk of the man who'd called me.

"I'm your Job Coach," he said. "Do you understand?"

I needed help until I could get another job—what was there to understand?

Despite not having slept well—panic in my dreams and a screaming Izzie dragged from my arms by men with shadowy faces, Lee-the-Landlord amongst them—I noticed there were no missing keys on his keyboard as I told him I had a three-and-a-half-year-old daughter and the two of us lived in a rented property.

He noted my date of birth and job history.

When he said, "Do you have any questions?" I asked him when—if I didn't get any of the jobs I'd applied for—I'd get some money.

"The first payment usually takes about five weeks to come through," he said. On autopilot added, "You can apply for an advance if you need to."

I was about to say I needed to when he said, "Wait, there's a problem."

When—running—I start to push myself, I feel as if my lungs are on fire. As if I'm going to have to stop and put my hands on my knees the way Denim Jacket had on Sainsbury's car park. But if I keep pushing something clicks into place and I feel as if I could keep going forever. My head clears and I feel calm.

Charging around Warley Woods, looking over at the trees, up at the sky, down at cracked slabs, I'd felt calm.

Yet when I returned to Edmunds Road thoughts were backed up, waiting for me.

Chief amongst them was that my Job Coach had said I wouldn't be able to get Jobseeker's Allowance until their investigation was concluded.

"Your investigation into Carl hasn't got anything to do with me and Izzy," I'd snapped.

"You're divorced?"

I'd shaken my head. "But we are separated!"

Fingers poised he'd sat with one hand on either side of his keyboard.

"We've been apart two years," I'd said.

"According to our records Carl Radford resides at 39 Edmunds Road," my Job Coach had insisted.

I'd said, "He doesn't live there, hasn't ever lived there!"

Without batting an eyelid, my Job Coach had said, "According to our records —"

I'd said, "Fuck your fucking records," and was escorted out of there.

Hours after my run I listened to Izzie tell how today they'd played games.

"Twister's my favourite," she said. Sounded as if she'd given it serious thought.

For tea, we were having jacket potatoes and tomatoes. She helped lay the table. Stepped back to inspect her work, then said, "Can we buy Twister?"

I couldn't remember the last time she'd asked for anything. Why I wanted to tell her we could.

Only I didn't have the money.

By this time seated at the table with her, when I cut open my jacket potato, I saw there was rot inside—a hard, dark ball of it.

Izzy saw it too, and when I sat back down after scraping it into the bin saw she'd put half her baked potato on my plate.

When we'd finished eating, using pages torn from an Argos catalogue as a makeshift mat and a wooden spoon as our spinner, we improvised a game of Twister and for a time Izzy's laughter made me forget I was an abandoned daughter, a cheated-on wife.

The following day there were even fewer jobs. Why after I left Bleakhouse Library I headed for the new TREVOR'S.

I said, "You once told me it's not what you know it's who you know. Do you know anybody who's looking for somebody?"

I shifted my weight from one foot to the other as Trevor Kennedy looked at the Post Office sorting depot fifty yards behind me. Was about to leave when he reached for one of the napkins stacked next to the ketchup.

I rang the number Trevor Kennedy had written on a napkin as soon as I got back to the house. When I had saw I had an hour before I needed to pick Izzy up—her place at Tots paid for until the end of the month. Planned to clean the kitchen and had a Jay cloth in one hand when the doorbell rang.

Convinced it was Lee-the-Landlord it occurred to me not to answer. But if I didn't maybe he'd let himself in rather than post another reminder. Deciding it was best not to let it come to that I opened the front door.

Denim Jacket wasn't wearing denim anymore and still I recognised him. In fact, I properly recognised him this time.

"Krish Sahota," I said. Naming Carl's go-to man for gear, nearly two years on recognised Carl's use had been out of hand long before we split, though at the time I'd been like a frog in water being brought slowly to the boil.

"I don't have any money," I said. His face still bruised from the beating he'd taken under the canal bridge he gave me a look which made it clear he didn't know what I was talking about. Gripping the edge of the door I said, "If Carl owes you, it's down to him. We split a long time ago."

"I heard," he said. "He split with Jaslin, too."

Jaslin Sahota was his sister. Gear what she and Carl had in common, with her where he'd been when he was supposed to be watching football with his friend George Douglas.

Krish Sahota said, "This's not about Carl. It's about you, Vicky. Billy Erickson's decided you're fighting Will Stepney."

"Tomlinson Windows started small," Eric Tomlinson said.

We sat in his office. Me on a hard-backed chair on one side of his desk, him—in an expensive suit—on a comfortable chair on the other side of it.

"But I monopolised on the market shift in '96 and here we are." He licked his lips and said, "Under the right circumstances I can create a budget for twenty hours a week of office cleaning."

I understood as much about what he meant by 'the right circumstances' as I did about the market shift of '96, but kept my mouth shut.

He said, "It'd be a self-employed position which'd advantage both of us."

If I got to ask a question the way you usually did in interviews, I'd ask Eric Tomlinson how—if I were a self-employed cleaner on twenty hours a week, minimum wage—it'd advantage me. But Eric Tomlinson didn't seem inclined to stop talking any time soon.

"One of the things I like about you, Vicky, is your attention to detail. Look how your blouse and trousers match."

They didn't. I'd put these trousers on only because they were so long, they hid my shabby ankle boots. He stood and came around to my side of the desk.

Twenty hours a week on minimum wage was never going to be enough long term but because I knew it was easier to get a job if you already had one, I was prepared to take it.

Suddenly standing beside me, Eric Tomlinson put his hand on my shoulder. I smelled his aftershave. Didn't recognise the brand, only that it was strong and made me want to gag.

He said, "In my experience a woman who pays attention to detail is a valuable commodity."

His hand made my skin crawl, but I held myself still until he let it slide forwards—

"Fuck off!" I stood up and shoved him so hard he had to step backwards to avoid going down.

First by the side of the canal and now here shoving fuck-heads something I was good at, it seemed.

Quickly recovered, Eric Tomlinson straightened up and said, "What do you think you're doing?"

I said, "What am I doing? What are you fucking doing—you just groped me!"

When he said, "You're delusional," I felt like driving my fists into his face.

Anticipating it, he took another step back and said, "I'll call Security."

My shabby ankle boots got me out of there in a hurry.

Once outside I turned my face skywards hoping the rain would wash away what'd just happened.

It was an old VHS tape. Its cardboard cover curled up at the edges.

Speaking as if he was talking about a stranger my old man said, "I wasn't a big puncher, but I was fast."

I watched him watching himself—the expression on his face tense —when I turned back to the screen saw him throw combinations and press forwards.

What he said about his speed was right, but before I could say so he said, "The winner was to get a crack at the British title," and hit pause.

As this memory replayed on a loop, I stepped into Kennings House, crossed the lobby to the lift and pressed the call button.

To ask for my old man's help felt like a betrayal of my mother but what else was I to do?

When he led the way through to the living room, I took in a thread-bare easy chair and a scarred drop-leaf table with half a dozen books stacked on it. My old man—I remembered—who'd taught me to read.

I said, "I need your help."

Here for the first time, I burned to ask him about the woman he'd left us for. What was her name? What did she look like? Would she step out of the bedroom at any moment?

"You want to sit?"

I shook my head. Told him about losing my job, what had happened underneath the canal bridge and being unable to get Universal Credit because Carl was being investigated though we weren't together anymore.

"Then Krish Sahota came to see me," I said.

Shifting the bulk of my weight from one foot to the other, I explained that Krish Sahota sold gear for Billy Erickson and the first time he came to my door I turned him down flat.

"But when he came back..."

I took £200 in twenties from my pocket and fanned out the notes as if they were playing cards.

Was it possible to age a year in seconds? My old man looked as if he had.

"Krish said when he told Erickson I'd shoved Smith's man into the canal Erickson started taunting him."

I put away the money.

"Erickson and Smith are top of the local supply chain. Do what they can to piss each other off but stop short of a turf war.

"Smith told Erickson there was no way a woman could push his man into the canal. Erickson told Smith not only was that the case, but he was willing to bet the woman could stay with his man if they went toe to toe."

Rearranging the plastic flowers in the pot before my mother's marble stone, I told myself they were better than nothing, though their colour had faded, the plastic become brittle.

"I'm sorry," I said. Remembered how if I asked my mother why my old man left when she was scrubbing a saucepan, she'd scrub harder. If I asked her when she was folding laundry, she'd apply so much pressure the veins in the backs of her hands bulged. I'd soon got the message and took for granted he'd left us for another woman. "I didn't know what else to do," I said.

Later, I planned to tour local industrial estates, knocking on doors to ask for work.

But first I hiked from the crematorium to meet my old man at Dave's Gym.

Owned by his old trainer, corner man and friend, a single storey building at the back of The Pheasant the gym stank of old sweat and leather.

At the far end was a boxing ring. Ahead of it were punch bags—all different sizes.

"The first time I set foot in here I was twelve years old," my old man said.

He sounded lost. In another life I'd have said something to help him find his way home. In this one, I watched him put down his sports bag and take from it a pair of leather mitts.

He said they'd let me hit as hard as I could without busting up my hands, then walked me over to a medium-sized bag and told me to throw jabs and crosses, the steady bap—bap of my fists against the punch bag immediately filling the gym.

When he called time on the punch bag, he nodded approvingly.

Sliding pads onto his hands he said, "You've got to hit and move." Paused to see that I understood, then came at me.

I soon sharpened up. The sound of my fists hitting bags or pads like the rat-tat-tat of a machine-gun.

On the downside, the £200 I'd taken from Billy Erickson was gone and I felt like I was standing on the edge of a cliff.

I wasn't. Was in Bleakhouse Library again: waiting for a computer sat at a table in the corner. Wasn't aware my old man was standing next to me until he said, "Carly Green broke her leg." Paused and said, "I told the caretaker I knew someone who could fill in, but if you're not interested..."

Already on my feet I said, "I'm interested."

Wearing corduroy trousers and a pullover with the sleeves rolled up the caretaker handed me a number #2 key.

It'd been years since I left Churchfields High School. Would the caretaker remember me? If he did, he gave no sign. My old man had warned me not to look directly at the badly fitting hairpiece he wore so I kept my eyes on his mouth.

"You wipe down the desks, hoover the floors and empty whatever's in the bins."

He peeled a bin bag from a roll as thick as his wrist and handed it to me.

"When it's full, tie it off and drop it into one of the Continentals on the rear car park."

When my first shift was finished, I stood by a window looking down at the yard. Jumped when—from the doorway—my old man said, "Looking at where you had that fight?"

I'd been thirteen when Abbie Guest grabbed my hair and yanked me towards her. Pulling Year 8 girls to their knees was her party piece and sharp —faced Abbie Guest's reputation was such that no Year 8 had ever thought to fight back. I hadn't thought to either, but when she yanked me towards her, I instinctively punched her and any appetite she had had for a fight vanished.

It was something I'd told my mother about, but my old man left us when I was in Year 5 and the fight happened when I was in Year 8, so how did he know about it?

He said, "Caretaker told me Carly's off for twelve weeks. The work's yours if you want it."

My question relegated to the back burner I told him I wanted it all right.

"I don't know how it happened," I said.

Didn't know either how I'd come to be talking about Carl. Was it gratitude or that we were outside The Plough—the place bringing back things I couldn't keep inside?

I heard myself say, "When I first met him Carl was funny," and my old man bowed his head. "But once he was using heavily..." Feeling the need to move, I pointed at the entrance.

Krish Sahota looked from me to my old man, sipped from a pint of Guinness and waited.

I said, "The fight's off. I'll pay back the £200 as soon as I can."

Krish Sahota shook his head. "You can't pull out."

I said, "Watch me."

Krish Sahota said, "Mr Erikson's been buying property."

Erikson investing in property came as no surprise, but I didn't see what it had to do with me fighting.

Registering my incomprehension Krish Sahota said, "There'll be an audience."

The moment my old man set eyes on Izzie, he stopped dead.

His reaction made her stop dead too. Holding a paintbrush thick with blue paint she stared at him whilst the other kids carried on painting, carried on chattering to each other, carried on chattering to Mandy Mizlocki —who on hands and knees expertly helped one of the Bailey twins shape a dolphin's fin.

Once her appraisal of my old man was completed, Izzie dunked her paintbrush into a jar of water.

Hearing the chink Mandy said, "Don't forget to take your painting."

Izzie carried it over to where we were standing.

"This is your grandad," I said, and with no hesitation, Izzie handed her painting to him.

When the three of us stepped into the hall—his voice barely a whisper —my old man said, "She looks just like your mother."

Izzie looked up at me. "I look like your mother?"

I said, "Yes."

She said, "Is that good?" I told her it was and managed to smile, though when we stepped outside was glad to be distracted by the wind pound-ing my face.

When Izzie said, "I want grandad to come for tea," I didn't speak until she yelped.

"What is it?"

She said, "You're holding my hand too tight."

Convinced that bringing him with me to collect her had been a mis-take I said I was sorry and loosened my grip.

Izzie said, "Did you hear what I said?"

Holding her hand with the lightest of touches, I repeated that I was sorry, but she shook her head.

"What I said before."

I nodded.

"You're coming to tea, grandad," she announced, then told him all about her day.

When she'd finished, she asked him where he'd hang her painting.

On the living room wall, he told her.

She asked him if he painted.

Not since he was at school—when Art was his favourite subject, he said.

As we ate, I listened as in answer to a further barrage of questions my old man told her he lived alone, didn't have a favourite TV programme, ran four or five times each week, read if he couldn't sleep.

Like that Art had been his favourite subject at school, this was all news to me.

"Let me wash up," he said when we'd finished eating.

I almost lashed him with questions of my own. Wanted to know who he'd left my mother and me for, where was she now and why he hadn't fought for the British Light-Middleweight title if he'd earned the right. Instead, I said, "I'll do it," pushed back my chair and scooped up our empty plates.

On the way out, he said he'd see me at the gym for our final session and was true to his word.

"If you don't hit him, you give him licence," he said as we worked. Said if I gave him license Stepney would hurt me. "What you did humiliated him. That makes him especially dangerous, but vulnerable too." He assured me if I kept hitting and moving, he wouldn't be able to find top gear. "Take no chances," he said with an edge to his voice. Flicked one of the pads at my head every time my chin came up.

After dropping Izzie off at Tots and cleaning my designated classrooms I slung the rucksack carrying my mitts on my back and waited for my old man to come up to me.

Thinking about what was to come, I imagined my nose broken, my front teeth knocked out. Cheered on by Ronnie Smith imagined Will Stepney kicking me as I lay unconscious on the floor.

Eventually, I went downstairs. Expected to see my old man on his hands and knees unblocking the hoover or some such but it wasn't the case.

"He was in a hurry," the caretaker said.

He frowned. Had I inadvertently glanced at his hairpiece?

"Are you alright?" he said.

My old man was supposed to be in my corner, but I told myself I shouldn't be surprised. "I'm fine," I said.

Despite the rain I stood staring at where the old TREVOR'S used to be. Would've stayed rooted to the spot if Krish Sahota hadn't stepped out of Key Services and waved me over.

All machinery removed, the place contained a hundred men, maybe more, the blue-painted steel walls bouncing their voices around. They sounded hungry. Figuring I was the main course I thought about pushing Krish Sahota out of the way and getting out of there. Knew I couldn't because Erickson'd be able to get to Izzie.

Erickson had WIN tattooed on the knuckles of one hand. BIG tattooed on the knuckles of the other. "Tall for a woman," he said as if I wasn't there.

"I told you," Krish Sahota said.

Erickson said, "Skinny though."

Will Stepney suddenly at the forefront of my mind, I turned.

Standing thirty yards away, he looked bigger than he had under the canal bridge. The eagle tattooed to his neck fiercer. Wore a vest to show off the weight—machine built muscles in his shoulders and arms. Flexing, he clearly wanted to prove to his boss and the men gathered here that what Krish Sahota said happened under the canal bridge couldn't possibly have happened.

Erickson said, "Anything less than 100% and you'll pay a price, girl."

When he strode away Krish Sahota said, "Have you come alone?"

It set me thinking about my old man again. Why had he helped me prepare only to bail on the day? Was he with his other woman? Was that it? I told myself he must be, and I was stupid not to have seen it coming.

"What does it look like?" I snapped.

Krish Sahota said, "Come on." The sound of hungry voices louder as I followed him.

Thick ropes were wrapped around steel bins to form a makeshift ring. I wore tracksuit bottoms and an old tee-shirt. My only pair of trainers. Watched by Stepney shrugged off my rucksack, took out the mitts and slipped them on.

Stepney wasn't wearing mitts. Seeing mine he turned questioningly to Smith, who called to Erickson, "What the fuck's this?"

Erickson said, "If your man can't handle it, I'll have her take them off."

Stepney sneered at that and climbed into the makeshift ring. The crowd surging forwards when he raised his fists and threw vicious—looking hooks at empty air.

When Krish Sahota lifted the middle rope for me the crowd moved closer still.

As if Marquis of Queensbury rules applied, someone rang a bell to start us off and Stepney rushed at me.

Chin glued to my upper chest I circled backwards as his shots pounded my shoulders and arms, the sound like distant gunfire.

Mouth open, Stepney soon sounded as if he was choking, though he continued to throw punches.

I told myself he'd slow and at that moment felt something cannon into the left side of my ribcage—what little oxygen was in my lungs exploded out. Black spots swarmed in my peripheral vision. Something thick gathered at the back of my throat.

"Hit and move," my old man called from my corner, urgency in his voice. "If you don't hit him, you're inviting him on," he explained.

Only he didn't. Because he wasn't with me. Had deserted me. Again. The bitterness I felt about that why for a moment I was tempted to disregard everything he'd taught me.

Thankfully, I didn't. Saw Stepney charging in again and fired a right jab, then a left cross into his face, one after the other, the sound like two pistol shots in a duel.

Blood spat from Stepney's nostrils and as one the men who'd bet on me to last a round roared.

When someone rang a bell to end the first round, I watched Stepney turn away, though even when he reached his corner I didn't move—gulping air held my ground at the centre of the ring.

"Over here," Krish Sahota called.

He held out a bottle of water. Was this an act of kindness? More likely it meant Erickson had bet on me to last some way into the second round, why though my throat burned with dryness I turned away and shuffled on the spot to stop lactic acid pooling in my thighs.

When the bell rang to start round two, I pressed my left elbow tight against the pain in my ribs and could've sworn I heard my old man's voice tell me to, "Close in on him, put doubt in his mind."

I caught Stepney under the left eye with a right jab, surprise then fury on his face.

If he'd tried, he could have avoided some of my shots, but to underline his contempt he chose not to.

My shots made him madder, and the madder he got the wilder the punches he threw. I was tired, but Stepney was suffering more. Seeing it I found myself thinking I'd get through the second round for sure. My mind on the prize of the next bell forgot to circle and felt a rope snap taut against my upper back, then a left hook slam into the side of my face.

I said, "I betrayed you. I did and I'm sorry but there was no one else I could turn to."

And through a smeary half—darkness heard my mother say, "I understand what you did and why you did it."

I said, "Do you?"

She said, "You've got Izzie to look after," and I was comforted, though for a moment only.

"You died before...How do you know her name...?"

Without warning my mother was gone and Izzie was speaking to me. Concern in her voice when she said, "Are you alright?"

I said, "I'm OK. Look what I bought you."

The concern in her voice replaced by excitement Izzie took what I held out to her and said, "Can we play right now?"

I said, "We can play soon," tasted blood and was suddenly conscious that I lay sprawled on the cold concrete floor, that the voices of the men gathered to watch me pummelled sounded hungrier, and Stepney was leaning over me, laughing.

No, I told myself, and moving quickly pushed with both arms. Stood, and threw a flurry of punches that killed Stepney's laughter.

A bell rang to end round two before he could gather his anger and came at me again.

"I win," Izzie said.

It must have looked painful when I smiled at her because she winced. I'd told her the swelling on my face was from accidentally whacking myself with the hoover at work and after she'd packed away our version of Twister—as she ate mashed potatoes and carrots—she told me about her day.

Tucked up in bed after her bath I read her a story and when she was asleep, I washed up, dried up, tied off a full bin bag.

Hampered by my bruised ribs I carried it out to the back yard and dropped it into the dustbin. Was on my way back to the kitchen when a thick envelope slid through the letterbox and plopped onto the hallway mat.

I froze.

Then—gathering myself—opened the front door.

Seeing there was nobody there I picked up the envelope and carried it through to the kitchen.

At the end of the second round, someone called my name. It wasn't Krish Sahota, though like him the caller held a bottle of water out to me. Who was he? How did he know my name? Maybe he heard Krish Sahota call me? I told myself that was it. Supposed he'd bet on me to last into the third round was why he was offering me water. Intended to hold my ground until he called me again. Something about the way he said my name what got me moving.

He said, "Rinse, don't swallow."

Was in his sixties with scar tissue above both eyebrows.

"Spit," he said, and jabbing with his chin indicated an area close to his feet.

I spat and saw strands of blood on the pitted concrete.

"Hit and move and he's there for the taking," he said when I handed back the water.

At that moment I knew he was neither some punter who'd bet on me to last into the third round or an ex-fighter with a heart. This was Dave Hennessey. My old man's corner-man, trainer, and friend. And I was torn between telling him I knew who he was and attacking him by proxy for my old man's absence until the bell rang to start the last round.

Stepney rushed from his corner. Only this time I didn't wait for him to reach me and start swinging. Met him at the centre of the ring and threw fast shots he once again refused to avoid, then circled away from his wild on-slaught.

Seeing he was already blowing hard, and his eyes were nearly popping out of his head with anger I darted in and did it again—the red blotches on his face testament to the fact that every shot landed.

My lungs burned and my muscles felt heavy, but I kept at it. Knew Stepney was still dangerous and if he set himself up and caught me properly it'd be over for me. But—dominated by humiliation—he didn't choose his shots carefully. Continued to throw wild punches.

His anger cost him the fight. The left cross I dug into his gut as he drew back his right ready to swing yet another wild hook at my head just a helping hand.

Stepney dropped to his knees. Eyes wide with disbelief crumpled in on himself like an abandoned toy at Tots.

There were jeers and catcalls as I backed away from him. Sweat sting-ing my eyes and running into my mouth.

Dave Hennessey called me over and I climbed through the ropes, peeled off the mitts, pushed them into my rucksack.

"Time to go," he said as—around me—men pushed and shoved angrily. "Get in."

Hennessey pointed to a white Punto.

"Do you need to go to A&E?"

I shook my head as he drove us past the train station and turned right at the lights.

Parked outside Tots I was about to get out when I turned to look at him and said, "Why did he send you instead of coming himself?"

It was almost dark in the little kitchen, but I didn't switch on the light. Sat thinking about how Hennessey told me when my old man had fought Ewan McKenzie in an eliminator for the British Light-Middleweight title it was stopped in the seventh, McKenzie counted out.

McKenzie never regained consciousness. Died a week later. Was twenty-six years old with a wife and a three-month-old baby son.

My old man didn't fight again but there was more to it.

Dave Hennessey had shaken his head. "There wasn't another woman, but he was convinced if he stayed, he'd ruin your lives after what'd happened."

A million thoughts spinning through my head I reached for the env-elope that'd plopped onto the hallway mat. Emptied it out and stared at the money.

Realising he'd bet on me to win, I remembered how when Proudy called him, my old man had told him I already amounted to something and always would.

"Alright," I whispered. Pressed the heels of my hands against my eyes and said it again.

Almost

"All trained personnel report to checkouts," ricochets from the aisles to the ceiling of Sainsbury's, Oldbury: whitewashed concrete pierced by rectangular glass panels painted California blue.

Docherty believes these glass panels have been put there to taunt her. Knows she won't feel the air on her face till her shift is over. Corrects herself: won't feel the air on her face till her shift is more than over since something that can't wait always comes along just as it's about to end, though tantalising glimpses of California blue and the impossibility of a prompt getaway pale into comparison with how—without warning—on this day like thousands of others, the voice of the checkout captain suddenly makes her feel.

She tries to wrap herself in indifference but fails. Why at the word "report" the hairs at the back of her neck come to attention and when she hears "to" she stops eating.

Others quickly finish their sandwiches, but Docherty can't. Feels as if what's in her mouth has turned to ash. Spits it into a paper tissue as she stands and is walking briskly away from the staff area when "checkouts" slashes at her, and—from behind—she hears sniggers.

As directed, the others turn right.

Meanwhile—with her head tilted forwards as if she's looking for something—Docherty turns left and when the checkout captain puts out another call, flinches and picks up her pace.

She makes it to the bathroom where—pinned like a butterfly by the fluorescents—she steps over sodden paper towels to get to the cubicles.

The checkout captain is a friend of hers, yet Docherty locks the door and when another call goes out—the sound pinging off faucets and tiles—and presses her hands against her ears.

It helps, but what if they come looking for her? Peer under the door and see her feet?

Hands clamped over her ears Docherty stands on the seat. Assures herself that now they won't be able to find her and when the voice of the checkout captain slashes at her again is oblivious to it—almost.

Driving Instructor Number #1

When Sarah was in the cutting-zone her concentration manifest itself as a squeezing together of her lips, and that morning as wisps of Julie's blonde hair exploded from her scissors her lips were practically welded together.

Such concentration spoke of a singular focus that was impenetrable. At least Julie had always assumed that to be the case.

Until now.

Now, Sarah stopped cutting and stepped back from the chair. Lowered her arms and carefully regarded Julie's reflection in the mirror.

Meanwhile, the noise of the salon continued unabashed. Sounds of driers, the clip of scissors, snippets of conversations all underpinned by a musical soundtrack. At this moment Take That chorusing, "I want you back, I want you back for good..."

Unable to withstand Sarah's unflinching scrutiny any longer, Julie said, "What?"

Using the tip of her tongue to break apart her welded lips, Sarah said, "That's exactly my question."

Acutely health conscious since the stillbirth of her second daughter, Julie hadn't smoked for six years, yet found herself longing for a cigarette.

"How long have we known each other?"

Julie frowned. "Ten years?"

"Plenty long enough for me to see something's bothering you, right?"

Take That had given way to Soft Cell singing 'Tainted Love' on an Eighties themed radio station Julie never listened to at home.

"Right," she said, fidgeting.

"So, spit it out."

"It's...difficult."

"Wait," Sarah said. When she returned was carrying two cups of coffee. "These're on me," she said. Salon policy that hot drinks and biscuits were priced separately from styling.

Julie brought her arms out from under the protective poncho to take her coffee. Sipped it immediately even though she knew it'd still be too hot.

After placing her scissors in the pocket of her apron, Sarah folded her arms. Stood an inch or so behind the chair in which Julie sat. Her gaze fixed on Julie's reflection. Only the right side of Julie's blonde hair cut. Her make-up immaculate as always.

"It's about David," Julie managed after another tentative sip of too hot coffee.

"That's a relief, I thought you were going to tell me you hated the way I cut your hair."

At least that brought a half-smile to Julie's face.

"What about him?"

Sarah's ex was serving time for his involvement with a fourteen-year-old boy who attended the youth club he had run two evenings a week. Something that'd made the front page of several of the tabloids. Julie wasn't in the salon at the time but had heard Sarah came in the day after the news broke and—hysterical, tears streaming down her cheeks and snot trailing from her nostrils—screamed, "Now you all fucking know!" If she hadn't been such an outstanding cutter—the best in Lucy's Salon, it was widely agreed—Lucy would've sacked her on the spot.

To call mentioning anything pertaining to Darren 'difficult' was to put it mildly. But Julie sipped more coffee— the temperature now about right —cleared her throat and in a voice pitched so that only Sarah would be able to hear her, said, "David hasn't...We haven't..." then shook her head brusquely and began again: "How did you know what the kid told the police about Darren was...true?"

Sarah turned to gaze out of the front window of the salon at people walking past in the bright sunshine.

"I know when people hear about such things, they always think the wife must have known all along, but I didn't. Our sex life was never very..." She shrugged. "But you get used to whatever's normal for you. I did. At least until our sex life became non-existent." She paused. Swallowed with difficulty. "Even then I thought it was my fault." She brought her gaze from the window and focused on her own reflection in the mirror. "I've never been much to look at." Julie opened her mouth to protest, but Sarah cut her off. "It's true, but so what? We can't all be film stars." She drew in a deep breath. Smiled faintly. "That's what my mom used to say." She looked at her own coffee, placed by the side of the sink, untouched. "Anyway, it'd been a while, so I thought I'd do something to get Darren's attention. There wasn't a lot to be done about my face, but I thought if I got the right kit..." She picked up her coffee, then changed her mind and put it back down again. "When that didn't work either I knew something was wrong and I was right...The police came a day later." She plucked her scissors from her pocket. Felt good with a pair of cutting scissors in her hand and was about to resume cutting when Julie spoke up:

"When you say 'kit'?"

A Talking Heads song was playing—'Road to Nowhere'.

"Ann Sommers," Sarah said. Looking Julie's reflection in the eye.

David didn't know how Yunus had got so close to him! When had it happened? Just as importantly: how had it happened? Alright, Yunus was pretty good, there was no denying it. But even with the tips David had passed onto him he wasn't special: was the driving instructor equivalent of a mid-table premiership team, no more!

And yet they were tied, there was no denying that, either!

Looking pointedly at the instructor league table pinned to the wall beside his desk for all to see, Carl had seemed pleased that—for once—David wasn't streets ahead of the rest. Why was that?

Awake at night David found himself searching his memories for some sleight, real or imagined. Something that he'd done or said to offend Carl that might account for Carl seeming so pleased by his apparent demise.

Nothing ever came to mind.

So why was Carl so pleased that Yunus was tied with him? Why?

Still answerless, David got out of the pale blue Skoda Fabia. Leaving the door open for Jason, he told himself it didn't matter. All that mattered was on the final day of their season it'd come to this: he and Yunus had the same number of first-time passes, the same number of first-time failures.

Yet it wasn't quite over. For he had a final test on the afternoon of the final day. And if Jason passed first time, he'd still be driving instructor number # 1!

Whereas if Jason failed...

With so much resting on the outcome, Jason wouldn't have been his first choice! His first choice would've been a learner in their late twenties. Nervous enough to be alert, but not so nervous they were shaking and unable to function properly. But he had no choice! Like it or not, Jason was his last chance to finish top of the table! Jason with his skinny wrists and penchant for brightly coloured shirts. Jason, who was still two months shy of his eighteenth birthday!

David was conscious of his heart beating too fast and hard. Knew the insurance for young male drivers was sky high with good reason. They were hotheads. Were practically drowning in their own testosterone. Eminently susceptible to a sudden rush of blood that made its way to their right foot!

"No speeding," he said.

Shit, Jason wasn't even behind the wheel yet and he was adding to the pressure on him! Adding to the pressure the learner about to be tested was under didn't help! All except rookie instructors knew that!

"Everything OK?" he said without missing a beat. Managed to smile. "Yeah."

What did that mean exactly? Was Jason—literally—perfectly fine and good to go? Or was it just evasion? A façade. Really, was he coming apart at the seams? About to implode. Ready to fail his test in no uncertain terms.

Managing to keep his own façade of a smile in place, David made his way around to the passenger side and got in.

Jason didn't slam the door.

David took it to be a sign that things were at least under some sort of control, though the shirt Jason was wearing today was bright red! Was that a warning sign? Did it signify danger? Mean he was fired up? About to ignite.

Stop it, just stop it! David told himself. Had to stop it because he knew that the secret—the great secret to first-time pass success—was the lesson immediately before the test.

It went without saying that the foundations had to have been laid prior to the pre-test lesson and if they weren't, no amount of last-minute fine-tuning in the pre-test lesson could rectify matters. But when the foundations had been securely laid—and David always did his utmost to ensure that they were, as did Yunus, he knew—the pre-test lesson made all the difference in the world.

Was this something he'd shared with Yunus?

Unseen by Jason, seemingly intent on driving all the blood from his fingers David made a fist of his left hand.

Had he shared this with Yunus?

"Jason," he said, he hoped calmly and reassuringly, "you're going to do everything just as you've been doing it for weeks now, and if you do, you'll pass first time."

And if you do, David thought, I'll still be driving instructor number #1 on Carl's league table. The instructor with the highest first-time pass rate. Me not Yunus the top dog at Pass First Time!

"Take the second exit at the island," he said. To his own ears at least still sounded calm. Still sounded reassuring, whilst imagining how it'd be for him if Jason failed.

If he finished second on the table would Carl mock him, reprimand him, get rid of him?

And what about Yunus? Would he make scathing comments and gloat? Yunus hadn't ever seemed that kind of person, but what if?

Beads of sweat formed on David's top lip. What about the other driving instructors? The rest of the Pass First Time team? Would he suddenly find himself alienated from them? Humiliated by them? A figure of fun?

"When I strike the dashboard with the flat of my hand, keeping control of the vehicle at all times I'd like you to execute an emergency stop," David said. Thought his voice still sounded calm and reassuring, though—worryingly—not as calm and reassuring as it'd been just a few minutes ago!

For weeks now—possibly longer—day and night he'd been relentlessly bludgeoned by torturous thoughts like these. Felt utterly estranged from Julie, from their daughter Erin, from himself. What if he wasn't driving instructor number #1 anymore? Even if Carl, even if Yunus, even if the other driving instructors said nothing it'd be there on the league table. An affront to him and how he thought of himself. Undeniable. Inescapable!

Certain that this day had been coming for weeks, David had found it impossible to think of anything else, fractured sleep and constant gut-ache new norms.

When had he last had an appetite? Any appetite?

Certainly, food seemed to have lost all taste. He ate only to survive, and digestion was a problem. What he ate instantly congealed into a solid lump. This the embodiment of his imminent, abject failure. What it'd feel like if he was no longer driving instructor number #1!

He slapped the dashboard and Jason braked—too late and too hard, nothing smooth about it!

It'd achieve nothing to castigate him. That much was obvious David knew, though less obvious to him at this moment was exactly how he should react. Should he calmly, matter-of-factly remind Jason of the correct procedure for bringing the vehicle to a halt in an emergency stop? The danger being that even if he was able to sound calm and matter of fact about it, Jason's confidence would be dinked and as a result he'd—

Fail!

Or should he elect to say nothing for fear of the damage his words might do to Jason's confidence only to have him assume what he'd done was correct?

When in fact if this was how he executed his next emergency stop he'd almost certainly—

Fail!

What should he do?

Inside his overheated brain that question and myriad failure-centric others circled like motorway hawks as David waited at the test centre, a leaden lump in his gut chastising him for being a failure-in-waiting.

David knew a driving test took—on average—forty-seven minutes. Red-shirted Jason had been gone for forty-five minutes and eleven seconds. Would he still be driving instructor number #1 in approximately one minute and forty-nine seconds' time?

Would he?

He laid a finger against his cold coffee cup as the world swirled about him and the pale blue Skoda Fabia turned off the A365 onto the car park of the test centre—

Well...would he?

Spandau Ballet played through the salon speakers as Julie took her seat before the sink and waited for Sarah to finish speaking to her previous customer and come over from the till—cleaning the blades of her scissors using a wedge of tissue as she walked.

When, finally, her eyes locked onto Julie's in the mirror above the sink, Sarah said, "So?"

Neither her expression nor her tone giving anything away, Julie said, "I went to Ann Sommers like you suggested...'"

Gripping her scissors tightly, Sarah waited.

Spandau Ballet yielded to Madonna.

'Into the Groove' was a song she'd always liked. Always been able to lose herself to. But not today. Able to wait no longer, Sarah said, "And did it work?"

"Well..." Julie said—

Clock-Radio

She dreams she's hugging him. Through his thin shirt feels the heat of his body. Against her neck feels the soft push of his breath.

"I'll miss you," he says.

At which point she comes gaspingly awake.

Usually—when the dream fades—she switches on the clock-radio and listens to the news on the hour.

Until it's time to get up and get ready for work.

But this morning she recalls how on the first anniversary of the disappearance an hour-long documentary was aired on TV.

Following it, a support group was formed for families and friends of the missing. Some who wanted wreckage to be found. Others who clung to a narrative in which ragged survivors were discovered on an obscure atoll.

This morning—though her eyes are open—she sees not the shuddering darkness of 5AM. Rather as fish drift by on soft currents sees the aircraft on the seabed. The fuselage intact though wings and tail have been sheared off.

Never able to believe the survivor narrative, she'd always wished the aircraft would be found until this moment.

Now, she draws fleeting comfort from the thought that what's left a thousand miles from land beneath a hundred feet of water, will never be found and slides out of bed.

Gets ready for work.

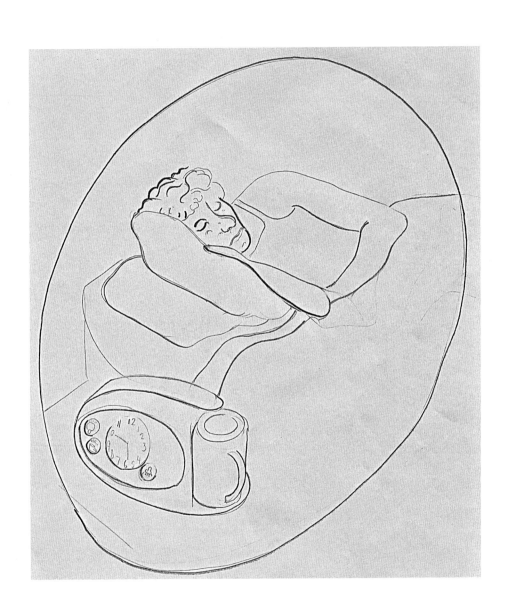

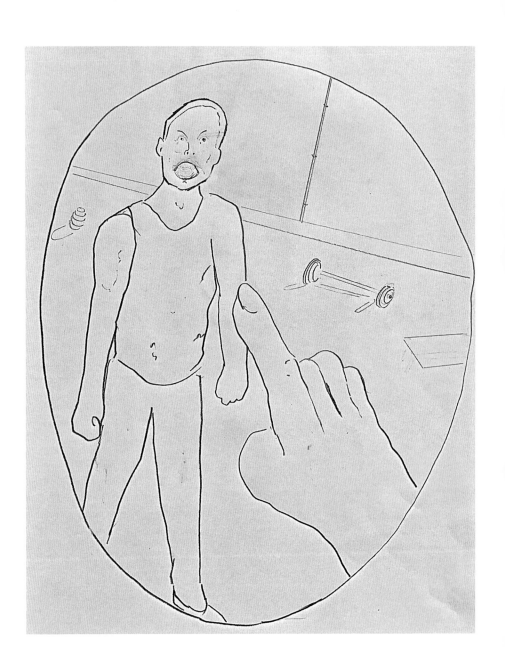

Lads

6

Some of the hair he'd grown to try and conceal premature balding flopping down over his eyes Tony Gould said, "This's a straightforward kidnapping." Which wasn't entirely true since he understood that straightforward kidnappings were for hard cash and this wasn't about hard cash! But to explain exactly what it was about was beyond him at this point. His eyes like piss-holes and his haemorrhoids giving it some. "I mean I'm not a paedo," Tony snapped.

The woman's mouth sagged open. Just the word 'paedo'—mentioned directly outside Lightwoods Primary School gates—what'd done it.

"Tony, isn't it?"

Blonde hair pinned back from her face with pink grips, faded blue jeans and a lot of gold on show, did he know her?

His question found its way onto his face and prompted her to say, "Your son's birthday party."

"You made the cake." Tony nodded. For Aaron's fifth birthday party, he remembered. A chocolate layer cake which Aaron ate so much of he threw up.

"How is Aaron?" She tried to smile but succeeded only in looking pained as her hands floated up to her hair. Seemed intent on adjusting her grips though they didn't need adjusting. The gold she wore reflecting afternoon light.

"He's fine," Tony said. Certainly, he hoped that was the case. Would've been happier if Aaron were with his grandmother but knew for a fact that slut Hayley would've gone there first.

Whereas the chances of her tracing down Jude—his sister Louise's ex—were next to nil. He narrowed his eyes and told himself what Louise had said about Jude and their two sons hadn't been proved: what Louise had said just her scoring points after the break-up: just her being bloody vindictive!

"Thanks for asking," Tony said.

And holding Freddie Cannon's kid's hand walked slowly away from the school gates. Thought he was going to get away with what he'd said since the cake lady's face was slack, her eyes unfocused.

Certainly, from the off a clean getaway was the way this had played out in his head. No tears from Freddie's kid. No sign of urgency until Freddie arrived and found his kid was gone.

After which there'd be urgency aplenty. Panic more like and it'd serve Freddie fucking right!

He knew Freddie would be late. Always was because the fucker did extra squats and even referred to himself as the 'King of Squats'—a nickname he hoped would catch on at Pro Fitness.

So far it hadn't, and Tony was glad. But right now—as things took a turn for the worse—it was the only thing he was glad about.

Suddenly, the cake lady's face lost its faraway look. Her eyes re-focused and she pointed at him and shrieked, "That's not his son! He's kidnapping him!"

He'd known from the moment it left his lips that it was a mistake to use the word 'kidnapping' but couldn't stand the thought of the cake lady entertaining even for one second that he was a paedo: needed to make clear that wasn't the case, no fucking way!

Now, Freddie wouldn't arrive at the school to find his kid gone. Wouldn't be suddenly riddled with white hot panic. Rushing round like a madman asking other parents if they'd seen his kid before chasing his questions into the school. Instead, Freddie would immediately be told someone had taken his kid. The 'someone' first described as a man wearing American grey sweats, then—courtesy of the cake lady—named.

There'd be no panic for Freddie Cannon. Meaning Tony's satisfaction would come only from knowing Freddie could never have imagined he'd take it this far. Cars, sheds, houses, even fucking wives, yes! But the line was drawn at kids, right?

Wrong! There were no fucking limits! There were only winners and losers, and he wasn't the loser because he'd shown that he wouldn't—ever—stop!

Lifting Freddie's kid into his arms and breaking into a run as waiting parents turned towards him, Tony Gould was disappointed things hadn't worked out as he'd envisaged. His disappointment sharpened by the screech of brakes.

Even before he turned, Tony knew Freddie had arrived and—aware that Freddie's kid was crying—broke into a full sprint. The school railings blurring, he turned without slowing and saw Freddie's Beamer—still bearing its scars—with the driver's side door wide open and the self-proclaimed 'King of Squats' gathering himself to give chase. The fucker so big that like a garden roller it took huge expenditure of energy to overcome initial inertia!

"Keep going," Tony panted to himself as he sprinted past watching parents and old Arthur the lollypop man.

5

It wasn't betrayal. It was something that had to be done.

"You're the mother of my kid, it's you I buy Valentine's cards for, only forgot twice in five years, right?" was what Freddie planned to tell Megan if she ever found out about this. Those exact words committed to memory. Readily accessible. Though of course his preference was for Meg to know nothing of what he was about to do.

What he was about to do had taken a lot of study. Homework how he thought of it and this the only time he'd ever been good at it.

The idea had come to him December 26th. When he was watching Groundhog Day. Comedies weren't his cup of tea. He preferred action. Something with Stallone or Schwarzenegger. Meg knew it and almost always accommodated him but had started watching it before he got back from training shoulders. Since the dinner she'd made was top notch Freddie decided it was the fair thing to do to let her keep watching. Sucking down a protein shake, he sat next to her—Meg blonde-haired and blue-eyed, as all his women had been.

"This's funny," Meg said. And as if illustration were needed, she laughed.

Stony-faced, Freddie didn't see what was funny. What he did see was how Bill Murray character's knowledge about people put him firmly in the driving seat.

It was why—for weeks his training curtailed—he'd studied Tony Gould's wife.

"What is it about me?" Hayley asked when he finally made his approach.

It wasn't her looks that was for sure. She was dark-haired and dark-eyed, dark hair and eyes—like comedy movies—things that hadn't ever been Freddie's cup of tea. Which helped. Compelled him to focus on Hayley as a person. No crafty looks at her legs even though she wore a short skirt and—in more ways than one—he was a leg man.

They were seated at one of the outside tables at Costa, Merry Hill. The shopping centre where—Mondays and Wednesdays—Hayley came for half an hour of window shopping before she went to work. Was always alone. Never went inside any of the shops and bought something and didn't ever stand so close to the windows that her reflection peered back at her, he'd noticed.

Firmly in the driving seat Freddie said, "You're lonely... Like me," a line he'd rehearsed so often he knew to lower his eyes as if he was about to cry when he delivered it.

His hand was wrapped tightly around his cup when Hayley's fingers grazed it. And when after rubbing the thumb of his free hand over where his eyebrows used to be, he saw tears budded in her dark eyes and knew it was in the bag so long as he didn't rush things at this stage and wasn't—afterwards —too pushy about requesting a photo of the two of them together...

Everybody knew Derek Rathbone was the man to train chest with. Derek a bona fide bench-pressing phenomenon. For his second crack at the Mr Universe even Mark Hammer, the owner of Pro Fitness, had benched with Derek.

Tony knew Freddie would bench with Derek every chance he got. Even immediately after a night shift. It was how he came to be waiting for Freddie at exactly the right time and was smart enough to park over the road from the gym with his headlights off. Directly opposite J's Scrap Yard.

Still sweating from his workout, his chest so big even his Range Rover could barely accommodate him, Derek drove off first.

Five minutes later Freddie followed the Beamer's headlights off the pitted Pro Fitness car park.

It was still dark and so cold Tony could see his breath even inside the Golf as—feeling like a movie private eye - he set off after the Beamer.

He drove onto Long Lane. Past The Stag to the island. Left at the island, then left again.

A three-bedroom semi with a block-paved drive, UPVC windows and front door, 39 Meadow Road absorbed Freddie Cannon.

Grinning, Tony headed back to The Stag. And after pulling up his hood so it hid his face, he walked back to Meadow Road: wanted Freddie to know it was him but didn't want witnesses who could put him in the dock.

The winter sky glistening, Tony made sure no one was watching. Not from number 39, not from any of the nearby houses. Unobserved, he passed his tongue over his lips and slid the spray paint from his back pocket.

FUCKER... WANKER... PRICK... TWAT... These were his favourite swearwords and Tony Gould applied them in uniform size—though varying order—to the previously immaculate UPVC frames, front door, and block-paved driveway. Muttered, "How do you like that King of fucking Squats?" as he stuffed the spray paint back into his pocket and—giggling—jogged back to his car.

3

Climbing the tree made him feel like a kid again, though not in a good way. To make matters worse his weight bent even the thickest of branches, but he couldn't exactly stroll into the man's back garden through the fucking gate!

Early evening, it was already fully dark: stars watching Freddie Cannon's awkward descent from the sycamore tree at the edge of the allotments with grim amusement.

Tony Gould's end-terrace house sat at the top of a narrow lawn bordered by un-loved panel fencing. Freddie saw there were lights on, though the curtains were drawn. Noted that even if a curtain were peeled back, he'd be hidden by the ten-foot-tall conifer at the top of the lawn.

Fucking sweet!

Freddie lowered himself from a branch overhanging the spiked railings. When he had, holding the petrol canister tight against his body, he checked the house again.

This time he spotted an attic room with a dormer window. A rectangle of yellow light leaking up into the night sky.

If anyone looked out through the dormer, they'd see him, no doubt about it! It was why Freddie hurried. Unscrewed the cap of the canister and advanced on the shed at the bottom of the garden with intent—the shed double-doored with a steeply pitched felt-covered roof.

Vigorously, he splashed petrol onto the wooden walls.

Dropping the canister to the ground, Freddie dug into his pockets whilst simultaneously re-checking the house—no one watching him from the dormer, thank fuck!

Lighter in hand, he leaned towards the shed. Brought the flickering flame towards the petrol-sodden timber—

It happened faster than he'd anticipated. A jagged spear of flame yanking off his eyebrows, scorching his cheeks, sucking all the air from his lungs.

Coughing violently, Freddie still didn't pause. As flames engulfed the shed and rose to pierce the night sky, he reached for the sycamore limb that'd facilitated his descent.

Twenty feet above the ground—his forearms burning with lactic acid —Freddie was convinced what he'd done would put an end it. Was sure that now Tony knew he knew where he lived, he wouldn't dare go on!

Panting as if he'd maxed out on a set of chins, he dropped from the tree into a potato patch and turned. Saw the flaming shed through spiked railings and broke into wild laughter.

2

Avoiding the potholes, Tony Gould strode over to Freddie Cannon's Beamer.

Brand new, the car shone. Not least because Freddie had it cleaned three times a week by the skinny, baseball-cap-wearing guy who worked the jet wash on the forecourt of Abbot's Tyres.

At Pro Fitness this was widely known. Several times Tony had heard Mark Hammer laugh and say, "Who has their car cleaned three times a week, man?" Heard Freddie laugh back at him and say, "The 'King of Squats' needs a car that's nice and clean."

The blue Beamer sat three yards from the road, waiting for Freddie to collect it.

Following their altercation Freddie had started his workout. Tony guessed he'd be mid-way through training triceps at this point.

Thirty yards away the skinny guy in the baseball cap directed his jet wash at a silver Merc. The sound blotting out Tony's approach to Freddie's Beamer and all his subsequent actions.

Casual about it—as if what he was doing was perfectly reasonable—Tony snapped off the Beamer's windscreen wipers and near-side wing mirror. Was surprised how little effort it took.

After laying the dismembered parts neatly on the bonnet Tony noted that the skinny guy in the baseball cap still hadn't looked over and no one passing by had seen anything, which was good news...

... Except it occurred to him that if no one saw him—in particular—do it, then Freddie mightn't automatically recognise the damage to his car for what it was—payback. Which wouldn't do, fuck no!

Tony stepped wide of another pothole. A lot of them on Abbot's Tyres frontage because old man Abbot believed maintenance of property was a waste of money. Why the wall separating it from Pro Fitness was in such a state of disrepair, too.

Reaching over, Tony wrenched one of the bricks from the top of the wall, as he'd thought the edges sharp - just the job.

With the swooshing of the jet-wash a counterpoint, Tony used the brick to score YOU LITTLE FUCKER onto the wing and passenger side door of the Beamer. When he was done placed the brick on the roof and stepped back to inspect his handiwork.

Now, Tony was sure Freddie would know exactly who was responsible and as he headed back to his Golf, grinned with the satisfaction of having settled things.

1

Many occupying spaces once given over to factories premises or shops, there were gyms throughout the Black Country. Most weren't up to scratch, but Pro Fitness was. Three times runner up at the Mr Universe Mark Hammer was deadly serious when he said, "Everything here's proper heavy duty."

It was why Tony Gould trained there. Knew the Universe was beyond him but thought he could take a local show someday and have his framed photo in reception with the other members who'd competed and won.

In his American grey sweats Tony was rowing with 100KG. Didn't hear the door to the gym ping as it opened. Was repping out when Freddie Cannon approached, these last reps the most painful in the set: what Mark

Hammer called, "Grow reps."

The muscles in his back screaming, Tony wasn't aware of Freddie Cannon's presence until he leaned close and yelled, "You little fucker!"

Slamming the bar onto the rubberised flooring, Tony straightened up and turned around—the mirrored walls showing three versions of his unmitigated disgust and the surprise on Freddie's face.

"Sorry," Freddie said—his voice loud enough to top a dance mix of Kylie's 'I Should Be So Lucky'.

Tony glared at him.

By way of explanation, Freddie said, "I thought you were Tommo."

Tony knew Freddie Cannon, Derek Rathbone and Tommy Macintosh trained legs together—such knowledge what might have prompted him to accept that an honest mistake had been made—Tommy Macintosh someone else who favoured American grey sweats—and let it go.

Except all the lads in the gym were looking at him. Which meant—from the corner of his eye he caught his reflected rear—they all fucking saw...

His chest and triceps were pretty good, and his back and biceps were coming on nicely, but by comparison his thighs were small. It was a common mistake easily rectified Mark Hammer had told him. Simply, he needed to squat. Tony told Mark he did squat. Mark shook his head and said, "Till your arse brushes the back of your ankles." And Mark was right. The extra depth had added size to Tony's thighs. But at the cost of haemorrhoids.

The leakage Tony had noticed was something none of the lads in the gym could've missed and was down to Freddie mistaking him for Tommy Macintosh, creeping up on him, calling him a 'little fucker.' Though kicking the shit out of Freddie wouldn't undo what'd been done—more precisely it wouldn't un-see what had been seen—kicking the shit out of him was—to his mind there was no doubt about it—absolutely fucking essential!

Re-framing his apology in the face of the anger he saw, Freddie smiled and said, "I mistook you for Tommo."

But Tony was having none of it and—able to read as much from the expression on his face—Mark Hammer drew in a deep breath.

His eyes boring into Freddie, Tony said, "You fucking prick!"

The apologetic smile fell from Freddie's face. The veins in his throat bulged. "What did you just call me?"

"A fucking prick," Tony repeated with relish. And—resisting the temptation to plaster one hand over the Australia-shaped red patch decorating the back of his American grey sweatpants—stepped threateningly towards Freddie—

At which point Mark Hammer snapped off the Kylie mix and yelled, "Whoa, whoa, whoa! Lads, not in the fucking gym! Anywhere but in the fucking gym!"

ard Points

Reward Points

He told James the pain was like someone slicing through his guts with secateurs and still James didn't stop laughing. They'd gone to school together, him and James. Been mates for a long time. Why—put out to put it mildly—Josh snapped, "'s not fucking funny!" Flecks of spittle spraying his phone.

James found the opposite to be the case. Through more laughter he said, "The blood went all over that woman's dress!"

Josh pressed his phone hard against his ear. Felt his face tighten and his jaw clench. It wasn't the blood! It was his fucking blood! How could James not understand that?

As if it would stall James' laughter, Josh spoke about the pain again. So acute it'd made him bend at the waist and gasp for breath.

That was when the coughing had started. A harsh, jagged sound that'd quickly consumed all conversations in The Barrel. At that moment Josh might have been all alone. All alone exactly how he'd felt when the blood came.

He said, "They had to give me two blood transfusions," and still James didn't stop laughing.

"I filmed it," James said with relish. "Everybody thinks it's great."

"Great?" The tightness in his stomach like when the ulcers had burst, Josh threw back the sheets and got out of bed. Felt as if his face were about to rip apart. Killed the call from James by dashing his phone against the bedside cabinet once, twice, three times.

Breathing hard but the tension in his face eased, Josh squatted and scraped the shattered phone parts into a pyramid-shaped pile. Then—after registering that the whites of the eyes of the man in the next bed were yolk-yellow—he got back into bed and shut his own eyes in the hope that he'd drift off to sleep.

Staring resolutely at the TV Josh's dad said, "This is the best quiz show since *Millionaire*."

As washed-out looking as he had been in hospital Josh braced his elbows against his knees as if gathering himself to contest this.

"But it wouldn't be if they got rid of Armstrong and Osman. Just as *Millionaire*'s nowhere near as good with Clarkson as it was with Tarrant."

Realising that he had neither the energy nor interest to contest anything Josh focused on his dad's profile—the sight of it what drove him to head off to the kitchen.

The once white paintwork was now as yellow as the eyes of the man who'd been in the bed next to his, he noticed.

Pushing the thought away Josh glanced at his mother. She looked as

43

if she'd been crying. But then hadn't she looked tearful since he'd moved back in?

"Why didn't you tell us you were living like that?" she'd asked as they drove from his bedsit with a car full of unwashed bedding and blood-stained clothes. Josh hadn't answered. Staring out the window at empty shop premises throughout the drive back home he'd wondered if his landlord—Danny Lee—would be able to track him down to collect unpaid rent and utilities.

Deciding only now that Lee almost certainly wouldn't, Josh opened the fridge and took out a can of John Smith's. Gulped it down as if he'd been walking for hours beneath a hot sun.

"What?"

"I didn't say anything."

"But you look as if you want to."

Josh dropped the empty can into the bin.

"I don't," his mother insisted.

There were bags under her eyes and cracks in her fingernails. She hadn't ever liked Carol and Josh had it in mind to ask why when she offered him something else to eat.

He wondered back through to the living room in a daze.

"Look." His dad used the remote to locate an episode of *Millionaire* with Clarkson at the helm as Josh lowered himself onto a chair and let his eyes rest on the screen. "You see that?" Without waiting for an answer Josh's dad said, "He's trying." Then flicked to an old episode of Millionaire. "Tarrant doesn't try. He's just funny. That's what's so great. I don't know anybody who thinks Clarkson's funny, do you?"

Josh hadn't given an answer and the question lay in wait. Jumped out at him in the middle of the interview.

"How would you deal with a difficult customer at your counter?" was the question he should have been wrestling with.

Yet had to fight down the impulse to say, "I don't know if Clarkson's funny or not and I don't give a shit!"

If he'd said it last night would his old man's saggy face have sagged even more? Unable to sleep, Josh had lain awake, watching the darkness dance above him, feeling as if he were suffocating. Would sticking his old posters back onto the bedroom walls help him sleep? Probably not. Besides which he wouldn't be able to. His mother had thrown them away. Or he had. One of the two. Either way they were long gone. Irretrievable. That word what'd compelled him to creep downstairs and—in darkness—drink another can of John Smith's. Gulping fiercely. Swallowing hard.

He'd drunk only two cans all evening, but it felt like more. His head fuzzy and his mouth bitter-tasting twelve hours later. Seeing that the interviewer was watching him steadily Josh tried to look as if he was giving the question serious consideration. When in truth he was further distracted. What if he was to vomit blood again? He'd been out of hospital a fortnight—during which time he'd drunk only two cans of beer—and still his stomach felt badly bruised, tender to the touch. He imagined blood—his blood—ricocheting off the desk between them and splattering his interviewer's pristine white shirt. Would the Tarrant of *Millionaire* laugh at such a sight? And what about Clarkson?

"Mr Price?"

Desperate to dislodge the bitter taste, Josh pushed his tongue around inside his mouth, frowned and said, "Did you just say: At my counter?"

Josh said, "I thought I was being interviewed to be a postman." Swallowed and said, "I couldn't work behind a counter to save my fucking life." Saw the stranger he'd spoken to turn away and nod along to an old ABBA song. Stepped away from the bar with his drink in hand and collided with Carol.

"Nearly drowned by a Jagerbomb," she said, her throat flushed.

"There are worse ways to go."

Carol smiled. Considered her very small, very white teeth her best feature. Why she smiled so often. Was still smiling when she said, "What you doing here?"

Josh could tell that Carol had been drinking, too. Her pupils the size of penny pieces. "Trying to decide if I should buy my ex-wife a drink," he said.

"You definitely should. I'm sitting over there." She pointed.

Placing her drink on the table Josh didn't know if he should join her or walk away. Her saying, "Seriously, what are you doing here?" what decided him.

He gulped Jager bomb, burped cautiously and said, "I don't know anybody who drinks in The Old Bush."

Carol finally stopped smiling. Raised her eyebrows and said, "You came here because you thought you wouldn't know anybody?"

"Yeah," he admitted.

"That's why I came here, too."

Josh touched his glass to hers and they drank. It being a weeknight the bar nearly empty, the barman watching Villa take a beating on a muted TV.

Shivering, Josh pushed through the chilled morning air to the bathroom. Was averting his gaze from the glittering arc of pus-yellow urine when he saw a man's razor.

Acutely conscious of the bruised feeling in his stomach, he carried it through to the bedroom between thumb and forefinger as if it were contaminated.

Carol pushed back the duvet and sat up. Peered through the grainy light at Josh in boxer shorts and said, "You've lost weight."

Despite that since his return to the family home his mother seemed intent on feeding him to death it was true, but Josh elected not to comment. Instead, he crossed to the window and drew back the swirly-patterned curtains. Saw the trees at the bottom of the garden fractured the sky, his upper arms covered by goose bumps watched a squirrel race along a high, horizontal branch and leap—

Carol said, "It's Nathan Sharp's."

Carefully, Josh placed the razor on the window ledge behind him and turned to face her. "You're seeing Nathan Sharp?"

"Somebody told him about us splitting up and he called me." As if she needed to prove it was really her, Carol used her fingertips to trace the line of her jaw.

His clothes lay in a tangled heap on the floor. Goose bumps spreading to his chest Josh stooped to gather them up. Pulling on black jeans that were a little too big for him he said, "I thought..." As he tugged on his shirt and struggled to button it vainly tried to decide just exactly what he did think.

"You thought that what happened last night meant we were going to get back together?" Carol offered. Rubbed at her eyes. Saw mascara on her fingers and sighed.

Josh yanked on his socks and stabbed first one foot then the other into his shoes.

Carol said, "I love you Josh and a part of me always will, but I'm not in love with you."

Leaving his shoelaces untied Josh straightened up. "What does that even mean?"

"It means you're selfish and I'm selfish and two selfish people don't belong together."

In the living room he saw an empty wine bottle and two glasses, one of them on its side, didn't remember drinking when they got back here though the way his stomach felt had no trouble believing that'd been the case.

Drawing her knees up to her chest Carol called out, "Nathan fucks around, always has." Able to hear Josh stumbling about downstairs, she struggled out of bed.

Trailing his shoelaces Josh almost stepped on Carol's upturned handbag—loose change and cigarettes scattered everywhere. The pain in his stomach sharpened by the movement he bent. Plucked Carol's supermarket loyalty card from the scattered detritus, pocketed it and kept moving.

Holding the duvet tight against her naked flesh Carol stood like a yeti on the landing. "But when he's with me..." She heard the front door open. Heard it close. She said, "...Nathan Sharp acts like the sun shines out of my arse!"

"You don't have to do the shopping," Josh's mother said.

Aware that the buttons on his shirt still weren't fastened properly Josh said, "Till my redundancy money runs out it's the least I can do."

His mother made out a list—her handwriting school girlish.

Her list what guided Josh along the aisles of Sainsbury's Oldbury with the shopping trolley fighting him every step of the way.

At the checkout he handed over Carol's loyalty card.

On autopilot the checkout woman said, "Would you like to redeem against the cost of your purchase?"

Grinning, Josh shook his head. Believed when he returned Carol's card and she saw the reward points he'd accumulated for her she'd realise he wasn't selfish. Not a fucking bit of it, and when she did...

Handing him back the loyalty card the checkout woman said, "Have a nice day."

The border at Pound rd

The Border at Pound Road

I think Eddie said, "Sandra's never coming back, is she?"
We were in his back garden on deckchairs stolen from a beach in Margate and he took a long pull on the joint he'd just lit and passed it over.

Admitting that Sandra wasn't ever coming back hurt like a blade going in, but Eddie found a radio station playing old songs and it seemed okay to tell him about the time we were cut off by the tide.

We'd got drunk and fallen asleep in the sun. When we woke our faces were burned. Seeing we were cut off, we sobered up quickly. Knowing there was no way we could climb the sheer rock face behind us I told Sandra we'd swim way out, past the headland, then cut left to make land.

"What else could we do?" I asked Eddie, a friend how I thought of him and why, I think, I went to him first.

When I told him what I had in mind Eddie looked at me as if I was a stranger. Somebody trying to sell him something cheap and nasty. Had he ever kept me standing at his front door before?

Putting all that aside I went over everything again. Though since he lived next door, I didn't understand why it was necessary for me to spell out to him that day and night the traffic didn't let up. Made it impossible to sleep for more than a couple of hours.

I said, "Imagine a fire inside your skull," and still Eddie acted as if he barely knew me.

Maybe he thought I didn't know about the crop he was cultivating and was afraid if he invited me in, I'd smell it. If that was the case, he was stupid on two counts. First, the time I talked to him about Sandra and me getting cut off by the tide, winking and grinning he confessed the joint we were sharing was "home grown." Second, I was his next-door neighbour. Meaning my only alternative to thinking he cultivated in his back bedroom was to believe that the constant hum I heard was him hoovering 24/7.

Eddie either didn't take on board that what I was saying needed to be done because his mind was on what he was cultivating or because he hadn't ever been my friend.

If that were the case it would account for why when I'd told him about Sandra and me being cut off, he hadn't asked how we managed to swim out past the headland.

I'd been too fucked up to think about it at the time.

Now, I decided it was the case that he hadn't asked because he didn't care how—with waves fizzing round our ankles—we'd been ready to try and swim though we pretty much knew for sure that we'd drown, when the tide turned, and we were able to simply walk out of the hole we'd found ourselves in.

I hadn't had sex in a long time and hoped it didn't show on my face when I knocked on her porch door and waited for Marian Clarke to answer.

Marian was eighty and her back was bent out of shape, but she still had fire in her belly, and I have a memory of her smiling when I told her what I thought needed to be done.

Sleeplessness was something she understood. She said whatever time she struggled out of bed to stretch the kinks out of her spine vehicles were charging up and down Pound Road. The racket something that set her nerves on edge and made her heartbeat fast.

"You're right," Marian had said, "We need to stop it. Let's get Jack on board."

Her husband was also over eighty but still sprightly. Sang in a choir at the Community Church at the top of Pound Road, that how—I think—we came to hold our residents' meeting there.

Following the meeting I made passports for all residents.

Posted Eddie's through his front door without bothering to knock and at ten to midnight was joined by Marian at the top of Pound Road—I think that it'd be the two of us who got the ball rolling something that'd been unanimously agreed at the meeting.

From a flask, Marion poured two cups of strong coffee. Handed one to me as I told her how not long ago when I took a train into Birmingham for a job interview, I saw my daughter on platform two at Smethwick Galton Bridge.

It'd been years since I saw her, but I recognised her immediately and waved to get her attention. But if she saw me, Louise gave no sign. Willing to get off the train even though it would mean missing my interview I pushed into the aisle but couldn't get past the people who'd just got on. The train started moving. Picked up speed quickly. As if my face was burned the way it was when me and Sandra fell asleep on that beach was how it felt when I looked out the window and couldn't see Louise anymore.

I think I told Marian this, though maybe I didn't because when I turned, she wasn't with me.

I was alone.

How had that happened when I was sure she'd been beside me just moments ago?

Only if she had been beside me where the fuck was the cup of coffee that she'd handed me?

Certainly, I badly needed a drink. My mouth dry and my throat parched—as if I'd been talking for hours.

Never mind, I told myself, convinced myself that it didn't matter that I was alone as a car approached and I stepped out into the road and waved my arms madly: ready—when the driver stopped—to demand to see their residents' passport if they were to pass the border into Pound Road.

Roofer

My Uncle Freddie got me a job with Henderson's Roofing. He told me I'd get used to it, but I never did—just ten feet off the ground and my guts would clench, my heart would race.

What I did get used to was hiding what I felt. Kept a straight face even when—standing right next to me—Billy Bartlett slipped and fell from the edge of a slate roof.

Billy Bartlett was fifty-two. Still on sick pay six months later, some of the crew said he was jammy, though the one-time I'd seen him since his fall he looked anything but. Seeing him—late and alone—limping out of the Bar of The Wheatsheaf, confirmed what I already knew: that roofing wasn't work that suited getting old.

It was why I had a plan.

Ostensibly to stretch, but really to get a better view of what would be my focal point, I stood.

I'd paint the trees as explosions of green. Would capture the essence of every leaf, the shimmering sky, and those old factories...

Roofer would be better than Cezanne's *Mont Sainte-Victoire*. Better than Van Gogh's *Olive Trees*. Would sell for fucking millions!

"Yes!"

"What d' you say, Callum?"

Ten feet away from me, Jayden Williams peppered corrugated steel panels with galvanised rivets.

Thinking quickly, I said, "I hope Chelsea fucking lose to West Brom tonight."

Jayden grinned, nodded, got back to work. Handled the riveter as if it was machine gun.

Meanwhile—near the edge—I studied the sky, nearby trees, empty factories. Was convinced that I'd paint them better than Cezanne. Better than Van Gogh. Yes!

opportunity

Opportunity

At first, I hated lockdown, which seemed to come right on top of my divorce.

Angie said, "Are me and Robbie finding somewhere else to live, or are you?"

Thinking it'd be the better option for him, I'd moved out. Though not long after Robbie got into a fight at school. Was small for his age but floored the other kid, then stamped on him. The whole thing captured on CCTV and used by the Head to exclude him.

Angie rang me and said, "Your fault," then hung up.

By then I'd moved into the gym I owned, Pro Fitness—every night rolled out a sleeping bag at the back of reception when everybody had finished their workout and gone home.

Even during lockdown, every day I mopped out changing rooms and showers, polished mirrors, and oiled cables on machines. Watched myself do these things. Me, Mark Hammer, fifty-four years old, three times Mr Universe runner up.

How long this went on for I have no idea. I wasn't sleeping well. Was wondering if I should try and get past the wall Robbie had put up to keep me out when I caught one of my old photos and knocked if off the wall.

It was of me hitting a double biceps during my last shot at the Mr Universe. I was thirty-five at the time and had trained harder than ever. Angie said I should've won, which meant a lot, but hadn't changed the result. Three second places, three times runner up, it got me thinking...

Now, I train six days a week—forty sets per body-part, like in the old days—and shovel down protein between workouts.

Regaining muscle is easier than gaining it in the first place, the mirrors testimony to that. My pecs, biceps, and quads growing fast, my abs reappearing, everywhere, veins close to the surface, pumped.

Next year's Mr Universe would surely go ahead. How would Angie and Robbie react when I took the title at fifty-five? My reflection smiled at me.

"Yeah," I whispered, and reached for a pair of 50K dumbbells.

Why I Did What I Did to My Dentist

If it wasn't toothache that kept me awake at night, it was the other renters crammed into 39 Stafford Street. Somebody was always coughing or snoring, though lack of sleep wasn't the only reason I was tired that day.

A puncture was what got the ball rolling and having pushed my bike most of the way into work I was late.

When I arrived, the supervisor gave me a look of disgust. Which is why I didn't tell him what had happened. Suspected that even if I did, he'd have done his usual trick of blowing out his cheeks and rolling his fucking eyes! The supervisor a man who earned three times what I earned, slept soundly, drove to work in a top of the range 4X4.

To make matters worse that day there was yet another full-scale re-organisation scheduled.

The supervisor said it was to do with "greater efficiency and increased profits." But then he always said the same thing and it couldn't have been right since every time Big Bertha—the operators' nickname for the photocopier that served all ten floors—was moved it cost £5,000! Constant costly re-organisation couldn't be the way to generate "greater efficiency and increased profits." We all knew it but none of us ever said so because one of the supervisor's favourite sayings was, "Operators should be seen and not heard."

Anyway, a full-scale re-organisation was scheduled and that wasn't all. Glaring at us, the supervisor made it clear that productivity mustn't be compromised, so we were still to take calls. Most of which—he insisted—could be dealt with without immediate access to a computer screen. He said some people weren't always looking at their screens when they should be anyway. Was convinced he'd never so much as glanced out of the window when he was an operator. Had always gone above and beyond the call of duty. Always going above and beyond the call of duty the reason why—the supervisor believed—he was the supervisor.

That day was spent lugging desktops and furniture in and out of offices whilst still taking calls.

If we couldn't deal with the problem the customer posed us on the hoof, we had to hike up to the top floor to use the laptops—the one item that during the various re-organisations had never been moved.

My working day was 8AM till 5PM with a lunchbreak spent in what was called the canteen, what was really two dispensing machines faced by a row of plastic chairs. Operators' contracts specified lunch was an hour. But I was the only operator who ever took the full hour. Every month there was a prize for the best employee. The supervisor hadn't ever won and I'm sure he blamed me because whenever I returned from lunch, he always blew out his cheeks and rolled his fucking eyes!

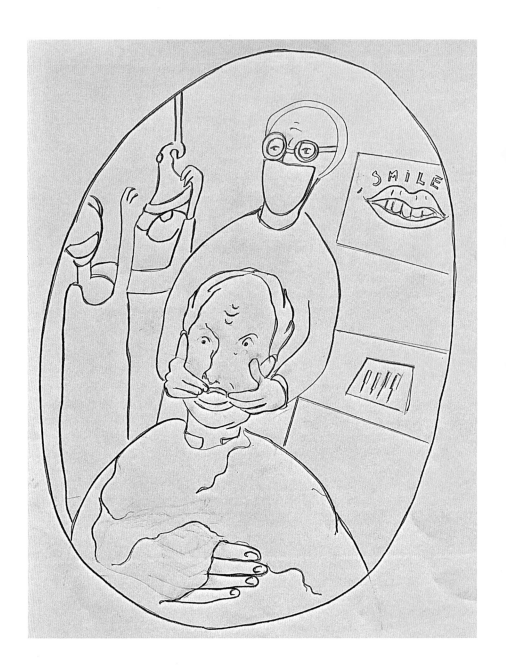

That morning I'd pushed my bike three miles to work, spent five hours lugging things in and out of offices, and hiked up to the laptops on the top floor half a dozen times. Lunch couldn't come soon enough, but when it finally did, I was too tired to eat. Sat slumped in one of the plastic chairs facing the dispensing machines—one selling hot drinks at a pound a pop, the other selling sandwiches that tasted as if they were filled with plastic.

The other operators were tired too. I saw it in their faces. But— somehow—they managed to gulp down something to eat and drink and get back to work after half an hour.

I took my allotted time and on cue when I returned the supervisor blew out his cheeks and rolled his fucking eyes!

Only that day he must have been more pissed off than usual about never winning employee of the month because he tapped his wristwatch with his forefinger, shook his head and muttered something about people "not taking responsibility."

I desperately wanted to speak up. Wasn't out of line and hadn't done anything wrong but didn't because I knew he wanted to replace me with someone who'd make do with a ten-minute lunch. Who'd do whatever the fuck it took for him to become employee of the month! So just clenched my jaw and got back to work.

I was the dentist's last appointment that day. Pushing my bike at a half-jog pace with the flat front tyre squeaking—as if it was laughing at me—I got there just in the nick of time. Would have had my appointment cancelled and still had to pay if I was more than ten minutes late—as per practice policy.

My dentist once asked me how I managed to keep so slim for a man my age. I told him I cycled everywhere. Had to. "Good for you," he said and smiled. And the funny thing—him being a dentist and all—was that he had terrible teeth. Teeth that were all discoloured and uneven. Something I'd always liked about him. My dentist someone I got on well with until that day.

That day my dentist told me I had cracks in my teeth from clenching my jaw. Told me that I should consider a mouth guard. Blinked and swallowed, then told me a mouth guard would help "curtail the damage." His blinking and swallowing was how I could tell he was working from a script. Giving me a sales pitch—as per practice policy. But my dentist telling me a mouth guard could "curtail the damage" to my cracked teeth isn't what upset me. Isn't what pushed me over the edge.

What he said next was what did it.

My head was pounding, and it felt like a layer of dirt had gathered under my skin and was demanding to be scratched out. Set free. I was hungry and thirsty to boot and the muscles in my legs were trembling as he blinked and swallowed again before telling me it was my "responsibility" to stop the hairline fractures in my teeth from getting worse.

At which point I found I couldn't stop myself—

Afterwards, I couldn't remember how I came to be holding my dentist's drill. Or how—as tired as I was that day—I'd been able to move so fast. Or how on earth I'd been strong enough to get my dentist down onto his dentist's chair and pin him there.

Afterwards, all I could remember clearly was how my poor dentist had screamed...

Today Next Year

No work today and still he woke before dawn. Chest tight, lungs screaming. Lie still, he told himself, and when that proved impossible pushed his tongue around inside his mouth as if something was hidden in there.

It didn't help, but then today it was always this way.

Making no noise, he dressed quickly.

His urine reeked of panic, and he brushed his teeth too hard, bloodying his gums.

He took the old tea tin from under the stairs, chose randomly before replacing it, and though there was time to eat, didn't, swallowed the blood in his mouth on his way to the car.

His sister always ushered him in and made him tea. When it was no longer possible for her to avoid saying something would tell him she didn't see the point of what he did. Didn't understand what he hoped to achieve by it. Always, then, he'd try to show her the photo he had with him and always she'd refuse to look, why he'd decided not to go and see her today.

The moon, low and to his left, urged him to go back to bed, back to sleep. He'd feel better if he did, but knew he couldn't, not today.

The roads were empty, yet he drove as if he were in heavy traffic as the moon paled and dipped. As the ribbon of light below it thickened.

It didn't take him long to get back here. He could have walked. Maybe next year he'd try that. Now, though, he brought the car to a halt. Saw that the house had been recently renovated and the front lawn replaced by a driveway but was sure a friend used to live here. If he knocked would Paul's parents answer—at first irritated to be disturbed so early, then pleased to see him? Was that how it would be?

He and Paul used to cycle to the nearby park. There they'd climb trees. His hands hoisting him high into the penetrating blue—when today it was all they could do to hold the steering wheel.

Pulling away from the kerb he drove along narrow roads. Dug at the brake when he saw Paul step out of the newsagents by their old school.

The car slewed to a halt. Never mind that it'd sound stupid or sentimental, he'd tell Paul that just a few minutes ago he'd stopped outside his old house. Would ask him if he remembered their ascents into the blue—

But there was no one outside the shop. How could Paul have disappeared so quickly a question he'd have dwelt on if a car hadn't drawn up behind him.

Over-revving, he drove quickly away.

When he reached the church, he parked and shut off the engine.

A truck passed by. Closely followed by a motorbike. After which the silence lengthened and grew weighty. Though tinged with grey the light seemed to bring out the red of the bricks, seemed to sharpen the spire. At last, he studied the photo he'd taken from the tea tin. Black and white—as most photos taken in 1955 would have been—it showed his mother and father arm in arm. Smiling for their posterity. Impossibly young, impossibly distant. He was sure this was the church where they'd been married, yet once again there was no sense of communion. No re-connection and therefore no point trying to speak of things left unspoken.

Never mind, he told himself.
On the anniversary of their death today next year he'd choose another photo from the tea tin. Maybe the photo of his father outside the steelworks. Though the steelworks were long gone, perhaps it would help that as a child he'd once witnessed red hot billets disgorged from a furnace, then shaped by men whose faces were smeared with sweat.

Perhaps, he told himself. Perhaps.

Yard for Rent

My brother saw the sign in the first place because he was working at the Select & Save on the Tipton Road. Told me the husband and wife who ran it had him unloading deliveries, stacking shelves, sweeping up.

"I'm a bloody dogsbody, but hey," he said, and shrugged. Was only two years older than me though it seemed more on account of how after the old man took off it was Dan who looked out for me.

Like the time in school when Hodgetts set against me. Hodgetts three years older and a head taller than me.

"What's your name?" he said.

It was lunchtime and we were at the back of the gym. Away from the main school building.

"Joe," I told him.

Hodgetts gave that some serious thought. "Your name's alright, but I don't like your face," he said. And started beating me.

Mom had too much on her plate to notice the bruises, but Dan asked me who'd done it. When I told him, he said I was to wait by the school gate at the end of the day. Was to nod when Hodgetts walked past me.

That day Dan followed him, and I went straight home so I don't know what happened. All I know is I didn't have any more trouble with Hodgetts. My older brother somebody who could sort things out.

Though he could never hold onto a job for long and when—in The Two Brewers—I asked him why that was he frowned and sipped his Carling. Swallowed and said he didn't know why, but maybe it was a thing of the past because working in Select & Save wasn't the worst job he'd had by a long shot. If packets of biscuits had been damaged, they let him take them. And if— even at reduced prices—they couldn't shift stuff that was past its sell by date he got to take it home for free.

"Ron and Jaspreet are okay," he said.

Yet a week later he asked me to come and look at a yard for rent on the Tipton Road.

Macy didn't say why she left me. "Figure it out for yourself," was as much as I ever got from her.

And having worked in the bakery for so long my mind was free, I tried to. Sometimes I imagined she said what she said because she didn't have a real reason. Other times I told myself she left me because of something I'd done.

Though more likely it was something I hadn't done. "You don't talk much, do you?" she said not long after we met. At first, she liked that I was quiet, though later it bugged her. With bloodshot eyes once snapped, "What're

you hiding?" I wasn't hiding anything. Told her not saying much was how it'd always been with me. "You talk to Dan," Macy countered. And since it sounded like an accusation, maybe I tried to explain why that was. Can't say for sure because this was around the time the shit hit the fan at work.

I hadn't seen redundancy coming. When the announcement was made stood in whites with the rest. The post-announcement silence unbroken until—recently returned after a run-in with cancer—Rakesh piped up.

"Mr Kendal? I don't get it. We make great bread here."

We waited while—not used to the bakery heat—Mr Kendall loosened his tie—his work suit way nicer than the one I was married in. "It's just the way it is," all he finally managed.

Dan pointed up at the sign and I took in that the yard was next to a tyre and exhaust place and recalled how when the last time we were out drinking I'd told him about my redundancy.

"What do you think?" he said. "Eh?"

How Goes the Way?

Today Fenton's sales are non-existent.

Even worse is that every caller hears him out then prevaricates.

As his caller right now is doing. Leaving him hanging. Like a fish on a line.

Zero still his sales score, seeing Shannon at the coffee machine two hours later, Fenton hurries over.

Immediately she sees him Shannon says, "You think I like you, but I don't," to Fenton's mind how she says it spelling out that she thinks he's a loser.

When he steps outside six hours later cold air slaps Fenton's face.

It's why seated at the bar of The George he gulps two pints of beer. Considers a third but decides against it. Is halfway home when he sees them outside Starbucks in the withering darkness. An old couple. Religious nuts of course but totally harmless unless he's very much mistaken.

Desperate to salvage something from the day Fenton heads towards them and the sign they have taped to their little wooden stand: *How Goes the Way?*

How goes the way?

"It goes badly," he says. Hands in pockets notes that nearby premises are closed, traffic's thinned, no one's walking by.

"The Devil spoke to me," he adds as if sharing a confidence.

"Where?"

The old man's question surprises him.

Finding it a pleasant surprise, Fenton decides to go with it so turns and points. Knows the alleyway's there because he went to school nearby. Hiked up to Big John's for lunch every day. Always had a slice of pizza and a Coke.

"Show us," the old woman says.

"Follow me," Fenton says. Waits as they pick up their sign.

Seeing the streetlight near the entrance to the alleyway is smashed, the darkness congealed, Fenton hesitates. This is the moment he could turn and walk away. Go home. Get something to eat. Sit slumped in front of the TV for a couple of hours.

Instead, he presses on. Intends to tell the old couple the Devil spoke to him over by the dumpster. Thinks that image is pleasingly poetic. If he can keep his face straight, will add that the Devil smells as if he's eaten at Big John's. Is sure Shannon will stop seeing him as a loser when she hears about this. Imagines the two of them laughing together. Shannon agreeing to go out with him sometime.

"Here we are."

The alleyway's narrower than Fenton remembers it and when he turns, he sees that the old couple are closer to him than he thought.

Disconcerted by their proximity and suddenly certain that Shannon won't be impressed after all, he's ready to let it go when the old man sets down their sign.

Fenton decides to come clean. Tell the old couple what he said about the Devil was just his idea of a joke. But all at once he understands this is no longer an option, though it's too dark to clearly see their faces recognises the old couple are not what he took them for.

Not even close to it.

They're nowhere near as old as he took them to be for a start. And there's deep-rooted anger in the set of their shoulders, the desire to inflict pain in every step they take. How could he have not seen it till now? Fenton's sorry and he wants to tell them so, but as the couple quickly close in on him sees it's too late for that, too. Too late to do anything but open his mouth and scream and then too late, even, for that—

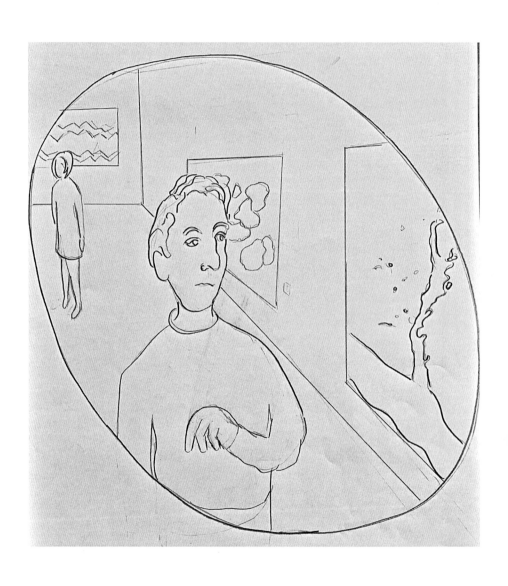

Notes from an Angry Man

'A Saturday night in January. Christmas decorations still up though they looked as if they'd been mugged and a group on after the bingo though the regulars weren't interested, and the secretary kept moaning about people chatting when the act was on.

'After he'd finished playing bingo my old man watched the group with a bored expression. Although he wasn't one of those the secretary had moaned about because he didn't chat. Preferred to concentrate on drinking. Could put away fourteen pints of Newcastle Brown Ale no problem.

'The three of us were squeezed round a wobbly little table. My mother chain-smoking, my old man swigging Newcastle Brown Ale and me—wearing a shirt with a collar so wide it practically touched my shoulders—sucking Coke through a bent straw.

'When they called last orders, my mother stubbed out her cigarette and my old man drained the last of his pint and stood up. Him standing a signal for us to do the same.

'The place emptied quickly. The three of us following the crowd through to the cloakroom. A Sports Argus and cigarette ash on the floor. My mother tugging at the hem of her skirt before going to collect our coats. Ferreting about in her handbag for the ticket stubs when the trouble started.

'Like me Bruce wore a wide-collared shirt. A picture of seventies-style elegance till my old man threw two punches—

'The dual-carriageway dips to the Birchley Island, encouraging you to speed and to make matters worse a Ford Focus undertook me.

'I'd been thinking about that Saturday night way back when, but now I accelerated and drew alongside the Focus. I pictured us stopped under the motorway bridge, traffic screaming past, the dark a solid block, saw the fucker try to get out and—

'But that's not what happened.

'"G-g-good evening, officer."

'"Should you be driving quickly in these conditions, sir?"

'Just nick me, I wanted to yell but didn't. Nor did I push the prick over into oncoming traffic. Knew I'd be caught and couldn't stand it. Enjoy freedom, fast cars, being able to stretch my legs whenever I feel like it. So, points on my license being the worst that could happen I kept my anger inside as he asked me how long I'd been driving and when I told him said it was long enough for me to know I should take extra care in wet conditions. Officer Adams made me feel like a stuttering kid in a wide-collared shirt. Asked me if I'd read the Highway Code recently. Kept me under his thumb the way fuckers in authority always do. Said I was a stupid, crippled, worthless little shit—just not in those words. And like a stupid, crippled, worthless little shit I sat there and took it.

'He let me off with a warning.

'Only I'd made my mind up I wasn't going to let him off.

'My old man's first punch broke Bruce's nose.

'The second caught him flush on the chin and he crashed to the floor, cigarette ash and the Sports Argus rising in sync.

'Bruce's brother muscled to the front and got my old man in a headlock. Like Bruce and my old man, Jack was strong because he'd spent his life doing physical work. There'd been times when the three of them swapped jokes and moaned about the hard graft they did for shitty pay—though my old man didn't get on well with Jack because Jack didn't like women—but for sure wasn't joking with either of them that night.

'Jack couldn't hold my old man for long. Nobody could. And with those crowded round parting like the Red Sea he threw Jack out onto the car park and would've kicked him to death if my mother hadn't hurried over and told him somebody'd called the rozzers.

'The next day I drove to the police station. Officer Adams arrived an hour later. Anybody looking at him then me would put their money on him but hadn't factored in my anger.

'I caught up with him when he was halfway to the station and handed him the Scotch. Had made up my mind I was going to go further than my old man had ever gone.

'When coppers pulled up alongside us, I thought they'd got him for sure. But my mother took charge. Could save my old man if no one else. When the nearest copper mentioned a fight at the Legion said we were the victims and if they wanted proof, they only had to look at her handbag, the handle snapped.

'It was after midnight when we got home, and my old man started drinking in earnest. Everything before just a warmup.

'My mother lit a fag and stood in the doorway of the kitchenette—never dreamt she'd die of cancer, her spine, and hips so brittle she was off her feet long before the end.

'"Come here," my old man hissed. Narrowed his eyes as I slouched over.

'I should've been in bed, asleep and dreaming.

'If only...

'"He got me in a headlock," my old man said—

'"What d' you do that for?" my mother yelled.

'I stared at the ceiling. Hadn't seen it coming because he was so fast. Noticed my mother's eye make-up looked as if it'd been dragged off in places.

68

'My old man looked down at me and said, "Don't ever let anybody put you in a headlock!"'

'Because he'd been bored all day was why near the row of garages opposite my house Bradshaw called Cammy a 'queer boy.''

'Usually, Cammy kept walking, but not that day. Cammy wasn't a friend of mine, but as Bradshaw passed, I heard myself say, "Leave him alone."

'"The fuck's it got to do with you?" Bradshaw snapped. Would've punched me if my mother hadn't opened the door and told him to clear off.

'When he'd gone, I crossed the road as if what'd happened wasn't worth mentioning to my old man.

'Fat fucking chance!

'Scotch in hand Officer Adams went into the station and came out with a crash helmet which he carried to where four motorbikes were parked in an area corralled by an aluminium rail. I watched him drive off, grinning at the thought of what I was going to do when I eventually caught up with him.

'I didn't hate my mother, but when she was dying found it easy to make excuses not to see her.

'She died in a makeshift bed because she couldn't get upstairs anymore. Her body like something you'd carry in a sack.

'After the funeral we sat staring at the indentations left by her makeshift bed and my old man told me she was 'lovely.'

'Maybe she was, but those indentations only brought to my mind what happened when she told my old man about Bradshaw.

'Coated with sweat he charged upstairs and stormed into my room. I was making a model. Was about to ask why he was pissed off when I found myself face down with plastic pieces of the Bismarck scattered everywhere.

'My face thick and hot in the shape of his hand, only when the swarming spots faded, did I see his lips moving.

'"Don't ever let anybody fuck with you," he said and opened his right hand as if to reveal a secret. Though it turned out there was nothing in it but the smoky dirt from Mansell & Booth's.

'Don't ever let anybody get you in a headlock or fuck with you—finally I got it.

'"Telling him was a mistake," my mother said later.

'Though I never quite forgave her and as I stared at those indentations felt I'd been right not to.

'In the Perry Hill Tavern, sitting alone Officer Adams drained a pint of lager.

'"Let me g-g-get you one," I said and reached for my wallet.

'My old man never let anything go, why a year after he came into my room and smashed my model of the Bismarck, he decided a test was in order.

'He wasn't at Mansell & Booth's anymore. Had a job at another factory that involved coming home filthy but finished early on Friday.

'How I came to be at the back of The George with him that afternoon.

'The kid who stepped onto the bowling-green had a football and wore a Villa scarf around his wrist. Asked if I wanted a kick about.

''After five minutes my old man called us over. Told the kid he could see he was better at football than me, but wanted to know if he was a better fighter, too.

'When the kid saw my old man wasn't kidding, he shoved me, hard.

'Cammy didn't say a dickey bird when I came between him and Bradshaw. Why six months later when I saw he was following me like a stray dog I took a detour.

'You had to cross the health clinic car park and jump over a knee-high brick wall to get to the back of the library. Where long grass and holly bushes hid everything from the street.

'I'd been shadowboxing every day. Knew how to get my balance right before I threw a punch and could throw combinations quickly, what I did to Cammy, boom, boom, boom—then watched him drop to his knees.

'What I'd done once I could do again. Knew the kid with the Villa scarf would drop as quickly as Cammy. His cockiness drained in an instant. But before I could execute, the kid's old man showed up. Saw my old man and opened his mouth. Was about to complain when the way my old man looked at him made him change his mind and he strode away, his son a pace behind.

'As if nothing had happened my old man asked me if I wanted a Coke when they were gone.

'I shook my head.

'"Maybe I should've got married," Officer Adams said. Refused to because he saw marriage as an act of conformity so let his woman walk.

'I took up boxing. My first bout at a sporting club in Kingswinford—rows of chairs spread out from the ring, the carpet blood red.

'In the changing room I stripped to my underwear and stepped onto the scales. Let a man in a wrinkled suit note my name and weight, a naked bulb shining on his glasses, fuzzy yellow blobs where his eyes should've been.

'When I stepped through the ropes the referee called me and my opponent to the centre of the ring, checked our gloves then sent us back to our corners.

'My lungs on fire I threw jabs, crosses, and hooks. The force of each punch such that I had to bite down on my gum-shield to keep my teeth from rattling.

'Halfway through the second round I dropped my opponent with a crisp left and watched the ref count him out. I'd won, only I didn't feel like a winner, not then and not a year later when I made it through to the quarterfinals of the A.B.A. championships where, way ahead on points I was piling in shots when I felt a sharp, hot pain in my left wrist—

'"You'd b-b-better not d-d-drive," I said to Officer Adams outside the Perry Hill Tavern. When I offered to drive him saw gratitude on his face. "Where do you live?" I said, though I knew. Followed my headlights as if they were my destiny.

'I wanted to take on my old man and before I broke my wrist in that A.B.A quarterfinal knew I was good enough.

'But things didn't work out that way. It should've been obvious it was just a matter of time before he had a heart attack, though when it happened, I was shocked.

'Afterwards, the veins in his arms were slack as unravelled wool and his great anger was gone.

'My old man got away from me, but Officer Adams wasn't going to be so lucky.

'"Come in and have a drink," Officer Adams said. Sepia-coloured prints of vintage cars on his walls.

'I wanted there to be music so maybe I was singing.

'If I was Officer Adams seemed not to notice. Was too busy switching on lights.

'Thirty years I'd waited for a moment like this. Now it'd arrived I wanted to laugh and cry at the same time.

'"A couple of nips of this'll warm us up." Officer Adams held up a bottle of Scotch. Maybe it was the one I gave him.

'I smiled as he carried glasses over. Kept smiling as I drove my fist into his face.

'Watching him try to get to his feet reminded me of when I saw a man who looked like me fall from his wheelchair and refuse to let anyone help him up.

'I stamped Officer Adams until my anger was gone.'

ADDENDUM

My father was a baker and for over forty years made his way down to the big oven.

By the time he opened for the men who worked the early shift the shop was filled by the smell of warm, fresh bread. A smell that still makes me think of dark streets and the clatter of work boots.

My mother said he worked too hard, and she was right. Less than a year after he retired, he had a stroke, following which she nursed him—my mother exceptionally kind.

'Williams shows himself capable of conveying emotions both sensitive and powerful, his work gentle and explosively unsettling...' is part of a review I clipped from the New York Times, still have. I was an art-therapist and painter. I'm gay. Can't recall a time in my life when that wasn't the case, though I married, and fathered a child.

We—I won't name her—shared an interest in Abstract Impressionism and during the Christmas vacation of our first master's year travelled to the US where we spent caffeine-fuelled days visiting galleries. Then hired a car to travel south, re-enacting a version of all the road movies we'd ever seen.

We shared motel rooms in which there were two single beds until one night only a double bed was available.

I knew I was gay, yet when she told me I made her happy, somehow convinced myself that I'd been mistaken.

Our child was born a year later, and I ought to have been happy, but felt like a stranger to myself.

Angus it was who organised my second exhibition and Angus it was, in the flat above his gallery expertly pressed his lips to mine, though I was a willing victim.

Wives find out. It's impossible for them not to. Laughable to think they won't. My wife found out and left. Taking our child. After which Angus couldn't bear to look at me anymore.

I had a nervous breakdown. Thought I'd never recover but slowly began to have fewer days when my chest felt so tight, I could barely breathe. Reached the point where I was able to think again. My first significant thought that I should become an art therapist. That how I came to meet Tony.

In his mid-forties but slim as a teen-aged boy he'd been referred with a long history of depression. I asked if he wanted tea. He said he did, with three sugars, and silently counted them as if he suspected I'd short-change him otherwise, after an hour said he had to be somewhere but returned the following day, picked up a pencil and began to draw.

The damage to his spine had severely impaired his motor responses and there were times when he was so frustrated, he'd put down his pencil and grip the arms of his wheelchair.

"It doesn't matter," I said.

But it mattered to him. Was why he stopped attending.

I left it a fortnight. Then went to see him. Saw framed, sepia-coloured prints of vintage cars on the walls when he opened the door.

"I knew it'd b-b-b-e you," he said.

Once our personal relationship began our professional relationship ended, though it was clear Tony needed help. When I suggested he might write rather than draw he looked hard at me.

"W-w-what should I write?"

"Whatever you need to," I told him, and promised that I wouldn't read of his fantasies till he was dead—though not that I wouldn't afterwards make clear what they were...

Spider Man #2

Runt came at me out of nowhere! Something in his hand. Not a bottle. Some sort of club, maybe. Never could've hit me that hard with his bare hands, no way! My little brother Dave a wimp his whole life, I swear! Came out of nowhere and whacked me with something. I didn't see it coming, that's the truth of it. Just felt it. BANG—and I was on the deck!

As if that wasn't enough the little runt put the boot in! Giving both kidneys and my kisser a dose! Blood and snot everywhere! Stopped only when he was too knackered to keep going! Lucky for me that he couldn't keep going very long. Wasn't fit enough. Hadn't been fit enough to play for the school football team when he was a still a kid.

Panting like an old man Dave bent over me and said, "You deserve that!"

Spitting out blood I sat up and said, "What did I do?"

"That Spider Man #2 you had when you were a kid," he said, still puffing and blowing, still bent over and red in the face, "If you'd not read it, if it was still pristine, we'd be quid's in, now."

Turns out the little runt had ducked into *Nostalgia and Comics* on Smallbrook Queensway to shelter from the rain and while he was in there found out what old Spider Man comics were worth, now.

Straightening up, still panting, he stormed off.

And yeah, alright, I could've gone after him and given him back some of what he'd given me. Would've done, too. In bloody spades, if it wasn't for the fact that he was right about that *Spider Man #2*... Shit, if I hadn't read it, it would've been worth a fortune, now.

By a River

Anderson's take on it was that if instead of talking so much the mechanic had done his job properly in the first place the filter would've been on tight. Wouldn't have come loose and dumped petrol over both carriageways when—7.30 AM: barely light and a fine drizzle falling—he was in the outside lane of the Birmingham New Road.

Where he remained stranded for over two hours. The stink of spilled petrol accusatory. Though when the tow truck eventually deposited him at Fast Fit Anderson made no accusation. Merely nodded when after fifteen minutes of work and without further explanation the mechanic assured him the filter was now, "100% solid!"

Was it, though?

Was it?

Anderson wanted to believe that it was but couldn't shake memories of being stranded, so remained rigidly in the slow lane with half an eye on the hard shoulder in case he needed to pull over.

Not that staying in the slow lane would automatically save him, he knew. The rapid thudding of his heart a counterpoint to the roar of traffic imagined losing power so suddenly he couldn't make it onto the hard shoulder. The driver of the lorry tailgating him failing to react in time and smashing into him at sixty miles an hour. The Astra crushed in an instant. Blood and bone exploded over the faded upholstery.

His grip on the steering wheel tightening, his knuckles turned white, uncertain whether to press his foot harder onto the accelerator or ease it off Anderson imagined his wife opening the front door and receiving the news of his death.

Erin would insist that the police were mistaken. Would ask why on earth he would've been on the motorway when work was only a few streets away. His shift waiting for him as usual. Just a normal day.

Such thoughts tempted Anderson to leave the motorway at the next exit. To make his way in to work. Telling his boss that he was late because he'd been snarled up in traffic. Forgetting this whole thing and getting his head down.

But seeing the sign for junction 3 he didn't signal and turn off. Rather, with his hands gripping the steering wheel even tighter he pressed on. This thing he was doing something that couldn't be put off, wouldn't be denied, didn't remember who'd invited him to the party, though was sure he had been invited: wouldn't have dared gate-crash even forty years ago.

Nearly Christmas, it was bitterly cold. The promise of snow in the air.

He hesitated outside the front door. Studying how the frost at the

a river

end of the drive reflected the streetlights he wondered if he'd made a mistake. Despite his invite felt he didn't belong anywhere near a house like this. Would've gone home if at that moment—her approach unheard—she hadn't said, "Are you going to knock, or am I?"

He turned to face her.

Had he seen her before? Did he know her already? Certainly, she seemed familiar to him. Intimately so. But before he could gather the courage to ask her, she said, "Come on," crisply knocked the front door and laced her free arm around his as if they were a couple.

Inside, the furniture pushed back to the edges of the room to make space, they danced—and for the first time in his life Ronnie Anderson felt truly alive.

Tingling with life how he felt hours later when—snowflakes spiralling out of the night sky—he walked her home. The two of them sharing secrets beneath the trees on Sycamore Road—where Wanda lived, back then.

Anderson signalled and exited the motorway at junction 12.

Still gripping the steering wheel tightly, for forty minutes he drove past graffiti-scarred industrial estates now bereft of industry and then along narrow residential streets.

Finally stopping, he manoeuvred into a space and got out of the car. Jammed his hands into his pockets and crossed to the river. With his head dipped as if he were a prisoner awaiting sentence he studied it intently, though the dark water steadfastly refused to surrender its secrets.

Finally tearing himself away, he turned to look at the houses facing the river and was suddenly filled with despair.

Until this moment, he'd expected Wanda's house to look just like the house she'd lived in on Sycamore Road.

Whereas none of them did.

His breath came in hard, sharp gasps—like cries for help.

Who had told him that—alone—Wanda had moved to live by a river? Who?

Slashed by the cold he admitted that he had no idea.

Did he even know the name of the street on which he was standing or the river running alongside it?

He didn't, no.

No...

He knew only that—forty years on—it was suddenly essential that he find her. Nothing more important to him. Noting. Why, closing his eyes, he breathlessly whispered her name and was gripped by a paralysing, intimate fury.

Seaside Towns

Seaside Towns

Feeling as if something had caught in his throat, he studied the stacked piles of newspapers. All that choice making his eyes ache.

He sucked in air that didn't taste right. Felt irritable. Stranded. Stood there for maybe thirty seconds, though it felt a lot longer. Time unspooling like a roll of film.

Couldn't remember the last time he'd stepped into *B & G Newsagents* much less the last time he'd bought a newspaper. For all he knew had lived his whole thirty-nine years without ever buying a fucking newspaper!

Until today merely bore witness to others buying newspapers.

Those he'd seen buying newspapers were usually men. On that he was prepared to put money. This the one fucking certainty in his day.

When they got home maybe they'd sit to read their newspapers with their legs crossed at the ankle. A radio on low in the background.

Something familiar like The Chi-Lites playing 'Have You Seen Her?'

If they lived with someone maybe they'd pause every so often. Comment on one of the stories they'd just read. Try and elicit a response. Get a discussion going.

Maybe even if they lived alone, they'd pause occasionally. Stare off into space before dipping their heads to continue reading.

Maybe, maybe, maybe!

Maybe was like looking down from a high ledge. A spiralling world of maybes no fucking good to him!

Certainties what he needed. Things he could rely on. Feel safe with. Draw comfort from.

Would being certain that most of the newspaper buying he'd bore witness to taken place on Sunday do?

It would, it seemed. For the spiralling slowed, then stopped.

Even his eye-ache seemed to ease a little.

Though it still didn't help him choose which fucking newspaper to buy!

He remembered Mollie telling him most newspapers were right wing. "And that's not us," she insisted.

This what decided him and why—as he waited to be served—his agitation dissipated.

Until he felt the shopkeeper's eyes come to rest on him.

Uncombed for weeks, was his hair wild? Was that why B or G was staring at him? Staring what it amounted to something else he was certain of.

Swallowing with difficulty he used his fingers to pat it down. Though the shopkeeper continued to stare.

Maybe it wasn't his hair. Maybe it was his clothes. They were clean,

79

but well past best. Everything faded. Worn. Trailing threads.

When the shopkeeper took the fiver and reached for his change he'd dash for the door.

But before he could, he saw the shopkeeper was staring at him again.

Only it was more than that. Now, the shopkeeper was staring and frowning at him.

He felt the world spiralling away again. And if it had ever truly backed off the fucking eye-ache was back. Would have preferred to exit whilst the shopkeeper was distracted but decided to stride from the counter and out the door anyway. No choice about it—much longer in here and his head would explode.

But before he could the shopkeeper said, "You look like Tim Roth."

Only the two of them in there and a drinks cooler humming away in the background.

"People must have mentioned it before, right?" Crucifying him with a smile the shopkeeper said, "In *Pulp Fiction* the scene where Tim Roth and Amanda Plummer hold up the diner's my favourite."

Had he backed out of there without saying anything at all?

Even as the door to B & G Newsagents hissed closed behind him, he couldn't recall. What had just happened difficult to get a hold of. Slippery to the touch.

He crossed to his car and got in. Tossed the newspaper onto the passenger seat and fed the key into the ignition. Oblivious to the rattle of the rusted exhaust exhaled deeply and thought about robbing the post office ATM.

He'd steal a car and mount the pavement at speed. Shoot past the post box on his left and slam into the ATM. The machine crumpling on impact. Crisp £10s and £20s exploding out. Fluttering like butterflies.

Carrying bin bags, he'd hurry over to the ATM. When they were full would run before anyone recognised him as happily married, Nut Factory employee Jay Hanson.

The money would buy him the time to complete his search. Begging what it felt like when he spoke to Ron Hunt. Disapproval writ large on the day shift foreman's face whenever he booked time off.

But it was stupid to choose the ATM of the post office at the top of the road where they lived.

And even if he chose to rob an ATM that was miles away could he steal a car? It looked easy in movies, but was it really?

No answers forthcoming, Hanson signalled and pulled away from the kerb. Drove down Pound Road. Passing their house on the left. Seeing his old school beyond it. Wondered why the place was called Oldbury College of Sport when it was still a school and why—over a hundred miles from the sea—

a row of deranged-looking seagulls eyed him from their perch above the main entrance.

Seeing nothing behind him he slowed. Was tempted to pull over and get out. Would the glare of a Tim Roth lookalike impel the seagulls to take flight? Electing not to put it to the test he sped up again. Needed the car ready for tomorrow.

At the bottom of Pound Road Hanson turned right onto the Wolverhampton Road and drove a quarter of a mile. Went through a set of traffic lights then turned right again. Through a break in the central reservation to get onto HiQ.

He parked in one of the bays earmarked for MOTs. Shut off the engine. Headed for Reception.

"Hello, young man."

It was a fucked-up thing to say. The mechanic was the young man. Not a grey hair in his head so far as Hanson could see. Whereas he had grey hair aplenty.

Except the bit about aplenty wasn't right. These days when he washed it, he straightened up to see the bathroom sink full of hairs.

Had that happened to his old man - was all that once thick, dark hair now long gone?

Hanson pushed the question away to consider another.

This one about the mechanic. Higgs, according to the breast pocket of his overalls. Was calling him a 'young man' a joke? Or was Higgs taking the fucking piss? Meaning it was right and proper that he show anger. Clenching the muscles on either side of his jaw as if he were crunching walnuts.

Unable to decide he settled for placing his car key on the counter and taking a half step back.

"Lovely," Higgs said. Smacked his lips as if he'd eaten something tart and said, "Have we got a contact number for you?"

"I'll wait."

Eyeing the well-used leather chairs in the far corner suspiciously Higgs said, "People don't usually."

Trying to look casual Hanson stood by the billboard at the edge of *HiQ*. Next to the traffic lights on Causeway Green Road. Directly over the road from the Hen & Chickens.

Only it wasn't the *Hen & Chickens* anymore. Was now a Chinese restaurant.

When had that happened? Though an early frost had been burned off by the sun the cold nipped spitefully at his fingers as Hanson told himself to forget it and opened his newspaper. Traffic on the Wolverhampton Road relentless. The sound like the roar of a wounded beast.

Blaming the noise for his inability to concentrate he gave up trying to read. Wedged the newspaper under his upper arm and gave himself over so fully to the endless flow of traffic he didn't notice Higgs' approach until the mechanic stopped a yard away from him.

His hair made cone-shaped by air blasted from a passing truck Higgs said, "Bad news, I'm afraid."

Whipping the newspaper from beneath his upper arm and rolling it tightly into the palm of his left-hand Hanson said, "It failed," as if it was something he'd expected.

"Big time."

"How much to get it through?"

Higgs said, "If I was you, I wouldn't bother."

"You're saying you can't do it?"

Seeing in Hanson's eyes what could be anger, what might be desperation Higgs said, "I'm saying you could pick up something newer for less than it'd cost."

Hanson gazed over at Bay 2.

The Polo was fifteen years old. A hatchback from 1984 with a sizeable dink on the nearside wing, myriad scratches on the paintwork, all the grey polyester seat and door trim faded almost white by the sun.

"That's not what I want."

Higgs said, "Your choice," and shrugged. His tight overalls raised to reveal a glimpse of Micky Mouse socks. A strange expression on his face.

Hours later Hanson saw a similar expression when he counted out what he owed in crisp £20s.

"You haven't robbed a bank, have you?"

If I robbed anything it'd be an ATM not a bank, Hanson thought but didn't say. Picked up his key and stepped outside. Daylight fading fast around the Polo's scarred black paintwork but traffic on the Wolverhampton Road still sounding fucking angry.

Up before it was light Hanson showered and dressed. Carried the Puma holdall he'd packed for his journey to the bottom of the stairs and placed it beside the *McVitie's Family Favourites* tin.

In near darkness he paused. Listened. The only discernible sound the steady beat of his own heart. Told himself that was good. Meant he hadn't disturbed Mollie.

What wasn't good was that he smelled damp. It rose from the cellar, bitter and clinging. Spelled out in no uncertain terms that during the recent heavy rainfall the cellar had flooded again. Drainage a perennial problem. The house an end-terrace built halfway down a hill.

Lit by torchlight Hanson had many times worked to clear a seepage drain blocked by mud sucked in from the garden at the front of the house. Panting with the effort yet chilled because the cellar was cold even during the dog days of summer filled bucket after bucket with mud. Hauling them outside to empty. A job that evidently needed to be tackled again. But not until he got back.

Hanson moved through to the kitchen. The once white walls now as yellow as the pages of an old paperback. Told himself when he returned—after he'd unblocked the seepage drain in the cellar - he'd plaster over the cracks and ask Mollie to pick out a new colour.

Pleased by his plan he nodded to himself. Spring the best time for such a job, he knew.

Mindful of light, it occurred to him that he should go further and get the mottled windowpane replaced.

After another bout of nodding set about making himself breakfast. A bowl of porridge followed by beans on toast more than he could comfortably eat. But remembered his old man saying, "Why spend a bloody fortune on food in cafes?" His broken nose wrinkling with disgust at the mere thought of café prices.

As a ribbon of daylight appeared above the kitchen roof of the house next door Hanson ate.

When he'd finished, he washed up and placed everything on the drying rack before returning to the hall.

Conscious of being overfull, he burped softly before poring over the well-worn pages of a roadmap. The MOT certificate stowed in the glove compartment. The Polo filled with petrol. Everything he needed for three days packed into the holdall.

Three days was all he had. Was due back at work at 8am on day four and knew if he wasn't Hunt would be on his case.

Hunt a man who pressed his overalls each day before coming in to work and had once asked him if he liked nuts.

Despite a dozen fluorescent lights and rectangular windows set eighteen inches below the ceiling the Nut Factory always seemed dark. And except for a one-week shutdown each year when the packing machines were serviced by a team of engineers, noisy to boot. The chug of machinery discernible as vibration in Hanson's fillings when he said, "I like nuts well enough."

"What does that even mean?"

Gauging from the way he lowered his chin that the foreman wasn't waiting for an answer he hadn't attempted to give one. Using alcohol wipes continued to remove oil and dust from the fixings at the base of the walnut packing machine until Hunt turned on his heels and strode away. Felt like racing over to him and putting a hand on his shoulder. Spinning him around sharply and saying, "You asking me if I like nuts? Seriously, Mr Hunt, what the fuck does *that* even mean?" Felt the words gather in his throat—hot and burning—and imagined the foreman's face as he spat them out. The thin lips pulled together tighter than ever.

Only Hanson hadn't said anything. Swallowed the burning words and kept digging at the nut oil and dust gathered at the base of the walnut packing machine with alcohol wipes.

Three days was all he had so he finished planning his route and selected cassettes for the journey.

Without taking his eyes from the road Hanson pushed in a tape cassette.

Listened to T Rex: 'Metal Guru' and 'Telegram Sam'.

Listened to Slade: 'Take Me Bak Ome' and 'Mama Weer All Crazee Now'.

Listened to Rod Stewart, Harry Nilson and Chicory Tip.

As he drove sang along to snatches of chorus—T Rex: *'Metal guru, is it you?'*—and odd lines inexplicably lodged in his mind—T Rex: *'Bobby's alright, Bobby's alright, He's a natural born poet.'* Wondered—as he sang—if what he remembered of these songs was from the first time of hearing as the three of them drove to Tenby.

Back then it would've been on a radio not a cassette player. Did that Triumph Herald even have a radio? Hanson frowned—a dozen lines suddenly chiselled deeply into his forehead—though it didn't help him remember.

He knew he'd sat in the back with a Marvel comic, the smell of burning oil and thoughts of a new TV show he'd recently watched. *Kung Fu*. David Carradine as Kwai Chang Caine being told: *"When you can take the pebble from my hand it is time for you to leave."* Didn't remember wearing a seat belt. Didn't think there were seat belts in the Herald. 72 when they went to Tenby, but the Herald a C reg from 65.

Leaning forwards, Hanson turned the volume way up and sang along, louder than before: "Moulded, I was folded, I was pre-form packed..." Chicory Tip. Was sure these songs were hits when he was eleven and that Tenby was his mother's choice.

A customer it was—a redhead, his mother had told him—mentioned the place to her. Said Tenby was lovely. Picturesque. With sandy beaches and a harbour. Nice little cafes. Shops that sold beads. The redhead someone who wore beads around her neck, wrists, and ankles.

Sandra's—the hairdressers where his mother worked—had often exerted an influence over her. Jay his name because when she was seven months pregnant his mother listened to a non-redheaded customer talking about her new boyfriend and liked the name.

Unlike the boyfriend, apparently. The customer saying, "He won't have it!" Insisted his self-proclaimed nickname be used.

"What's his nickname?" his mother had asked.

Winking into the mirror the customer had said, "Elvis."

His mother had stopped cutting and—scissors poised mid-air asked if the boyfriend looked anything like the real Elvis.

The customer's response had been to laugh and shake her head.

Hanson had a headful of Sandra's stories but knew the hairdressers where his mother worked wasn't there anymore because not long after her funeral—Mollie accompanying him, Mollie never far away during the year it took from the day of her diagnosis for his mother to die—they went looking for the place.

Sandra's used to be across the road from *The George*—where his old man played cards, all smiles when he returned with a pocketful of cash—and adjoined *Abbot's*. Run by Mrs Abbot. Who seemed ancient though she knit at a furious pace. The click of her knitting needles like machine gun fire. *Abbot's* a place where you could buy one ball of wool at a time if that was all you could afford. One ball of wool at a time how his mother used to knit jumpers for him and his old man, Hanson remembered.

He also remembered that as well as *Sandra's* and *Abbot's* there'd been a butcher's shop—*Bert's*—and a DIY place—*Dennis Hall's*. He thought there'd been a greengrocer, too, but couldn't for the life of him recall what it was called.

The shops were all long gone anyway. Demolished to make space for a mini supermarket with an ATM beside the entrance.

The ATM not one he'd ever contemplated ram-raiding.

Hanson told himself it didn't matter that he couldn't remember the name of the greengrocer. Yet wondered if there was a photo of it buried in one of the albums he kept in the top of his wardrobe.

He didn't think so.

But there were plenty of photos of his mother from that time.

Mostly black and white they showed her as a dyed platinum blonde. Though there was no mention of Marilyn on her memorial. *June Elizabeth Hanson—1940-1990—"Simply the best"* it said on account of her abandoning Marilyn in favour of Tina Turner when the old man left. Hid her big hands whenever the camera clicked, of course.

Continuing to drive, Hanson sang: "You wear it well. A little old-fashioned but that's all right..." Rod Stewart.

After which—his own big hands tight on the steering wheel—he grew silent.

The sky was full of cracks, and it wasn't the only thing. Why were the roads in such a bloody state? It felt as if someone was drumming inside the car. A heavy, arrhythmic beat that filled his skull and brought back yesterday's eye-ache.

Yet he didn't slow. If anything, he drove faster. His face clenched like a fist told himself things would be better when he made it to Tenby. Held tight to that thought and remained oblivious to the worsening rattle of the exhaust till the tail end fell off. An arc of sparks spraying from under the chassis as he pulled into a layby.

Hanson shut off the engine and pressed his head against the headrest. Waited for his breathing to steady, then got out.

Traffic zipping past, he studied the trees backing the layby—naked branches fracturing the already cracked sky—before squatting down to see that the muffler was still attached but barely. The clamp hanging from a single bolt.

The words unbidden he sang: *'Hey, hey, hey, look wot you dun to me...'* Slade.

Did so until he noticed a van selling hot drinks and snacks parked thirty yards away. The eyes of the owner on him—Big Derek stitched onto a baseball cap worn backwards. Watched as Big Derek disappeared from the service hatch and appeared outside a moment later. Stepped over to a pair of stocks beside his van, raised the board, placed his feet beneath it, then lowered it and sat looking at him.

Hanson turned around.

But there was no one behind him. Just him and Big Derek in the layby.

Having no other choice Hanson walked over. Saw that the stocks had been made recently and as if trying to backstroke out of them Big Derek was flapping his Hi Tecs back and forth. Followed his gaze and saw a grey plastic bucket at the far end of the stocks. A few coins at the bottom of it. Immediately dug into his pocket, pulled out a handful of coins and tossed them clatteringly in with the rest.

Grinning, Big Derek released himself and stood up.

Was a head shorter than Hanson, who said, "Bloody exhaust came off."

His right hand out the side window of the rescue truck and his fingers wriggling like seaweed through the rushing air Martin Griffiths said, "Last year Del spent a month dressed as a goldfish."

Hanson made a show of looking impressed. Considered mentioning that he didn't understand how the exhaust could fall off when he had a fucking day-old MOT certificate in the dashboard of the Polo but chose not to. Instead, focused on the empty Coke cans and *Mars Bar* wrappers packed tightly between the dashboard and windscreen. A life story of sorts.

Turning away to look out at roadside hedges blurring past he found himself thinking about other life stories.

"I stayed at a pub one weekend when me and your old man went fishing on the Severn," his Uncle Kevin had told him.

Hanson no more than nine or ten at the time.

"The landlord said I was the best customer he'd ever had."

Uncle Kevin made no secret of the fact that he could down a dozen pints of *M & B* in a single sitting. Afternoon or night. The Saturday night before Christmas when he'd tried to kill his wife, Jenny.

Early Sunday morning had been when Hanson heard his old man telling his mother what'd happened. The old man's voice hushed, but not enough.

"Kev said he finished a bottle of *Johnnie Walker* when we got back from the Legion."

It was raining softly. The patter on his bedroom window a counterpoint to his old man's words.

"When she came down from putting the kids to bed, he asked her if she was screwing the Treasurer. Said I'd told him she was."

Lying on his side Hanson drew his knees up to his chest and slowed his breathing.

"Jenny told him not to be silly. I'm not fucking silly, he said and hit her."

Making no noise Hanson had swallowed. Wished he could stop listening and shut it all out but couldn't.

"He kicked her from the front room into the hall. Would've kicked her to death right then and there if Lauren hadn't come to the top of the stairs."

Lauren the youngest of Kevin's two girls. Blonde hair and blue eyes. Not much bigger than a doll.

"He put her back to bed and went downstairs to carry on where he'd left off."

Hanson had kept his back to the bedroom door in case his mother pushed it open to check on him.

"But Jenny was gone. Somehow, she got the front door open and crawled outside. Crawled under the hedge and banged on the neighbour's door."

Rain had continued to patter against his bedroom window.

When Hanson caught up with him, he planned to ask his old man if it was true that he'd told his brother Jenny was screwing the Treasurer of the Legion.

Hoped his old man would say it wasn't.

Jenny divorced Kevin and a year or so later Lauren was run over and killed. A broken doll what his mind's eye took him to when he thought of it. The head smashed but one of the heavy-lidded eyes still open.

Hanson wanted to know if his old man had ever seen his brother again. This another of a fucking shitload of questions he burned to ask when he caught up with him. Sat him down and looked him in the eye.

"When you can take the pebble from my hand..." Kung Fu.

To Hanson the word landlady suggested someone who was old. Wore a Victorian dress. Had her hair in a bun. Held a lantern as she led the way up a narrow staircase and down a long corridor.

Whereas the landlady of *The Apostle* B & B was younger than him. Wore black jeans and a drop shoulder jumper. Had her hair cut short. Didn't carry a lantern or flick a switch because there was no need. Plenty of light pouring through the centre pivot roof window in the loft bedroom.

"Just the one night you said?"

"That's right," Hanson agreed. Through the pivot roof window saw Tenby Harbour. The pink- yellow- and blue-painted Georgian townhouses on Crackwell Street and part of Castle Beach beyond. To *The Apostle* B & B had carried his holdall, the *McVitie's Family Favourites* tin and an assurance from Griffiths that the Polo would be ready first thing tomorrow morning. A new exhaust fitted, good to go.

Middle of the Road came at him. Sally Carr's voice clear as a mountain stream: *'Just a little bit lonely...'*

Working to push aside a nagging doubt that the Polo wouldn't be ready Hanson turned to the landlady and said, "It's a great view." Paused, then added, "Picturesque."

'...Just a little bit sad...'

Turning from the view he put down his holdall and the *McVitie's Family Favourites* tin. Took out his wallet. Hoped paying her would allay any suspicions she might have about him. Something funny in her voice when she'd asked him if he was staying for one night only.

Seeing the crisp notes, he hoped she wouldn't ask him if he'd robbed a bank.

Thankfully that was the case. She folded the money into her jeans' pocket though still didn't seem at ease.

Had the sight of the biscuit tin unnerved her? He pointed and said, "I bought along some photos." Smiled and saw her smile back at him but to his mind not convincingly.

'...Oh Soley Soley...'

"I'll leave you to it," she said.

Maybe she'd said something else, too. Maybe just before she stepped out of the attic room, she said something about it being nice to see him again.

Listening to the silence, Hanson told himself he had to be mistaken. Had never seen her before and hadn't been to Tenby since 72.

On Cracknell Street he paused to shuffle through the photos he'd selected from the *McVitie's Family Favourites* tin.

Set off again only once each of the images was fixed sharply in his mind. The photos in colour but being far brighter than it bore little relation to reality. In them his mother wore a floral maxi dress and platform shoes. His old man wore flared jeans and a patterned shirt with a shoulder-width collar. In one photo had a cigarette in his mouth, though Hanson didn't remember him smoking. Maybe the cigarette was a joke? Certainly, his old man was smiling. The gap in his two front teeth visible.

He stopped opposite number 37. The house luminous blue. The number wrought iron.

It'd been twenty-seven years since he took a picture outside this house. At least Hanson assumed he'd taken the picture. Had no memory of holding the camera, framing the shot, but so what? Assured himself no one remembered taking photos. They just snapped—and that was it. The resultant picture what encapsulated the moment. Brighter than reality or not became the memory.

The photo he assumed he'd taken was of his mother with her arm around his old man's waist.

'...*Soley*...'

The photo taken on a summer day. His old man so darkly tanned the rose tattoos on his forearms were barely discernible. His tattoos acquired while he was stationed in Germany on National Service, though he had no memory of having it done, he'd said and winked and laughed.

'...*Soley*...'

The pair of them were smiling. But was the fact that his old man hadn't put his arm around his mother a sign of things to come? Deep-rooted difficulties between them even then. The years before he left just a shoring up. Their life together a fucking lie.

When he caught up with his old man Hanson would ask.

But now—twenty-seven years on from when it hit number 1—uninvited, David Cassidy's voice filled his head: '*How can I be sure, in a world that's constantly changing?*'

Trying to dislodge the words, he rang the bell of number 37 and heard a dissonant chime deep in the house.

It seemed important to decide his first words before the door opened. "Is Joseph Hanson here?" Why not just that? Followed by, "I'm his son, Jay

Hanson."

If whoever answered asked to see proof, he had his driving licence in his wallet alongside the crisp tens and twenties he'd bought along for the trip.

Only he mustn't think of it that way. A trip was somewhere you went to walk on a beach, swim in the sea, take all the time you wanted to drink a cup of coffee. This wasn't that. A fucking search what it was. To find his old man why he'd come to Tenby and why—if he couldn't find him here—he'd drive to Barmouth. Why if he couldn't find him there either he'd drive to Llandudno.

So, when the door opened, he should say, "I'm searching for Joseph Hanson."

But hearing footsteps approaching on the hard-floored hallway of number 37 he turned and hurried away.

He reached the harbour in no time at all. Stood alone at the edge of the jetty and looked over at the boats. Some with sails, some with motors. All surrounded by rhythmically bobbing buoys.

One photo showed his old man climbing the rusted iron rungs of the jetty. As if he'd just disembarked from the *Light of Pembrokeshire*. Though that wasn't the case. Was just the impression he wished to give. Something staged. Had taken three or four steps down from the jetty, then glanced over his shoulder as if giving the *Pembrokeshire* a final thanks for his safe return from the sea.

Squinting against the afternoon sunlight Hanson studied the names of the boats in the harbour. Intent on seeing if the *Pembrokeshire* was still moored here.

It wasn't. Which he experienced as disappointment. Sharp. Bitter tasting.

Disappointment's bitter taste was what drove him to ask the barman in *The Three Mariners* if the *Pembrokeshire* moored somewhere else these days.

White shirt, shaved head, the barman said, "No idea, but if you come through to the Bar you can ask Gareth."

Gareth Stokes eased the pool cue across his bridge hand. The subsequent click of balls like the chink of wineglasses.

Home to the smell of cigar smoke the Bar was smaller than the Lounge. Barely enough room for pool table and two old men nursing pints of bitter. Each with a foot placed on the tarnished brass rail fronting the bar like cowboys washed in from a long drive.

Cowboys suddenly at the front of his mind, Hanson remembered To *Tame a Land*. The first Louis L'Amour Western he ever read and always his favourite. Thought of the yellow-paged edition back at the house waiting to be reread in some impossible future until Stokes took up his attention. Sixty-three what Hanson took him to be. The same age as his old man. Though as the 8-ball dropped into the top right corner bag and Stokes straightened up and smiled he saw there was no gap between his two front teeth.

"You were unlucky," Stokes said.

It wasn't true. He hadn't played in years and had never been any good in the first place.

Stokes said his dad left *The Dragon Slayer* to him. Said she was a Day Sailor. Said there weren't many of them in the UK and he didn't understand why that was. Never had. Said they raced Day Sailors in the States and Brazil all the time. Said Uffa Fox was the designer as if the name would mean something to him.

Surprisingly, it did. Hanson recalled his old man pointing at a boat moored in the harbour and telling him Fox had designed it, though not whether he'd said it in Tenby, Barmouth or Llandudno.

Nor did he know why his old man would have known such a thing. The old man a painter and decorator who after a couple of pints told anybody who'd listen that he wanted to be a Bingo caller.

Maybe the knowledge was just something he'd picked up along the way.

Unless boats had really meant something to him? But if they did, he hadn't ever mentioned it. The staged photo the closest he ever got to revealing a secret nautical passion.

The name Uffa Fox meant something to Hanson, but he gave no sign of it as Stokes stunned a stripe into the bottom corner pocket and admitted he hadn't ever raced The Dragon Slayer himself. Had only ever used her for pleasure.

"Six-foot beam. Seventeen feet long. Fiberglass hull."

After trickling the 8-ball in at an acute angle Stokes looked properly at Hanson for the first time. Saw he wore khaki trousers, a blue lumberjack shirt, a dark coat, none of it in very good nick.

And that he was intense looking.

"What did you say you did again?" Hanson hadn't said and Stokes didn't wait for him to, now. Placed his cue on the table and said, "You're the guy who robs the diner at the start of Pulp Fiction, right?"

"Right," Hanson said. Managed to smile as Stokes stepped over to one of the circular tables flanking the bar, sipped his Guinness and gave him the once over again.

He thought Stokes was about to ask him why he wanted to know about the *Pembrokeshire* and felt his heart quicken. Had the photo of his old man climbing down from the jetty and the words he'd prepared when he rang the door of number 37 ready but still felt nervous. Dodged Stokes' further scrutiny by turning to look at the two men at the bar.

Though he couldn't drink like his brother, his old man had always been a drinker. Meaning that if he was in Tenby, he'd surely be somewhere like *The Three Mariners.*

Could be one of the men at the bar for all he knew.

Before Hanson could rule it out Stokes started speaking again. His voice quieter than before. Its intimacy what turned him.

"Rhys and Michael took the Pride out most weekends. They'd placed top five in a couple of races and got a taste for it." Stokes raised his Guinness to his lips, then changed his mind and put it down. His eyes fixed on Hanson – gripping a pool cue as if the game were still in progress – Stokes said, "One Sunday morning they went out and didn't come back. Coastguard found what was left of the Pride three days later." He took two deep breaths and said, "None of the investigation team was ready to say so, but when she was towed in, I knew a bloody sub had hit her. Sheared off her rudder and put a big hole in her hull."

Hours later Hanson lay staring up at the darkness in the loft bedroom of *The Apostle* B & B. Unable to sleep he'd at first been incapable of putting Rhys and Michael's final moments from his mind, then couldn't stop thinking about his mother's death. Without Mollie knew he wouldn't have been able to cope as the cancer ate her, with the agonising chaos of interminable hospital visits and his mother's inability to accept what was happening to her, with his own unutterable rage at his old man not being there when he was most needed.

Restless and sure his tossing and turning would wake everyone else in the house Hanson threw back the duvet and eased out of bed. Careful to make no noise he dressed in darkness. Picked up his holdall and the *McVitie's Family Favourites* tin and descended the stairs on tiptoe. Let himself out into the wind-chilled darkness and deposited the key he'd been given in the steel box attached to the wall beside the front door.

He walked without sense of direction or time. The darkness swaying tidally. Glad of the cold until it yielded its power to distract him.

When that happened Hanson found himself avidly searching the empty streets. Gripped by the certainty that at any moment—looking just as he'd looked in the photos—he'd see his old man leaning against a wall or seated on a doorstep as if waiting for him.

'Metal guru, is it you? Metal guru is it true...' T Rex.

Continuing his search, he revised how his old man would look. At sixty-three would surely be wearing corduroy trousers and a vee-neck jumper. His white hair mostly gone. Deep lines arcing from his nostrils. Bracketing his thin lips.

Hanson's eyes ached. His throat burned.

'...Metal guru could it be...'

Working his way back from the harbour he wondered why—if he was in Tenby—his old man would be out in the middle of the night.

No answer forthcoming, he still searched until hazy grey light began to fill the sky.

At which point he headed for *Griffiths Autos*.

Seeing the place wasn't open yet he circled back to the harbour and sat on a bench with his holdall beside him. The *McVitie's Family Favourites* tin on his lap.

'*...All alone without a telephone...*'

Driving, Hanson told himself that the landlady of *The Apostle* B & B hadn't said that it was nice to see him again. Rather she'd said it *would be* nice to see him again. Touting for business what she was doing. Something she probably did with all her customers. Nothing to sweat about.

When he left Tenby, the sun was out, the sky was blue.

Now, cloud cover was heavy and the promise of rain afoot.

But at least traffic was light as he pushed in a new tape: hits from '73.

Listened to Bowie: 'Jean Genie'.

Listened to Paul McCartney & Wings: 'C Moon'.

Listened to Carly Simon: 'You're So Vain'.

Others.

Today he didn't sing along even though he knew these songs better than the songs he'd played yesterday. Twelve going on thirteen when he'd first heard them.

Twelve going on thirteen an age when he hadn't questioned any of his old man's advice though he questioned it now.

Was it better to go hungry than buy food from a café?

"Fuck no!"

He planned to stop to eat as soon as he saw somewhere suitable.

But first he'd Dinas Mawddwy to climb. Dropping the Polo from second to first gear as Wizzard played 'See My Baby Jive' glanced over to his left and saw an RAF jet paralleling the contours of the valley.

The jet beside him.

Then ahead of him.

Then accelerating out of the valley—away and gone.

Elvis sang 'Always on My Mind' as he crested the hill and began to descend, quickly gearing up, the road unwinding rapidly before him, the tyres humming, the beauty of Snowdonia offered up before him like a sacrifice.

Had he noticed its beauty back in '73 when he was twelve going on thirteen? Maybe. But probably not because his head was buried in a comic book as it had been on the way to Tenby the year before.

'*You were always on my mind...*'

Seeing a café, Hanson signalled and pulled off the A470. Not the shortest route he could have taken though it may have been the route his old man used. Remembered his mother's anxiety about the steepness of the climb up Dinas Mawddwy and his old man's bullish counters. Their roles always fully rehearsed. No cue ever missed. And by his old man no stone ever left unthrown.

Hanson parked. Lack of sleep made it hard to judge how long he'd been driving. Thought he'd played his way through three tapes and was some way through a fourth. David Essex singing: Rock On when he hit Stop.

It had been early when he set off from Tenby, yet it looked like it'd be well into the afternoon before he reached Barmouth.

When he did, he'd grab some sleep in the car before resuming his search. Barmouth smaller than Tenby how he remembered it so a couple of hours of searching all it'd take.

Certainly, he didn't plan to stay overnight. Late afternoon or early evening planned to leave Barmouth. Set off for Llandudno. Maybe stay overnight in a layby. Spend the money saved on accommodation on something nice for Mollie for their anniversary – just a few days away.

Or maybe he wouldn't even push on to Llandudno at all.

Maybe he'd head back home.

Maybe that'd be for the best. Recharge his batteries before facing the disapproval of the dayshift foreman. Hunt always harder to bear after a break from routine. As if his immunity had been impaired.

The more Hanson thought of it the more it made sense to curtail his search.

Maybe he shouldn't even push onto Barmouth.

Maybe he should head home today. And not just because he was tired and a day of rest before facing Hunt would do him good. Having had a replacement exhaust fitted he'd already spent more than he'd anticipated. Far fewer of the crisp notes left in his wallet than he'd have liked.

Intending to finalise the decision once he'd eaten, he crossed the car park. Passed two parked lorries on the way. Up close saw the cafe was modelled on an American diner.

Stools were fixed in place before a counter. Booths before each of the roadside windows. Red the dominant colour.

Two lorry drivers sat with an empty stool between them eating BLT sandwiches. One wore a donkey jacket. The other a denim jacket with the collar turned up. Neither turned when Hanson stepped inside the café and slid into the booth nearest the door. A laminated menu on the table. Serviettes jutting from a plastic vase.

He couldn't remember when he'd last sat in a café. Without too much thought had settled on a BLT for himself when the woman slipped into the seat opposite him.

'See my baby jive...' Wizzard.

"I need you to help me," she said quietly.

"...just to see my baby jive..."

Hanson hadn't heard her come into the café. Hadn't heard the door hiss closed behind her. Judged her to be in her early thirties. Shoulder length blonde hair. Dark eyes. Wore an olive-coloured waterproof jacket that buried her. The left side of her face red and swollen.

'...ate all the razors while pullin' the waiters...' Bowie.

"What can I get you?"

Disconcerted by the appearance of the waitress Hanson flexed his fingers as if he was about to shuffle through the photos in the *McVitie's Family Favourites* tin again.

"Mug of tea and a BLT, please."

Rings on every finger and both thumbs the waitress scribbled onto her notepad.

Hanson watched the woman opposite touch the swelling on her face with her fingertips.

'...your hat strategically tipped below one eye, your scarf it was apricot...' Carly Simon.

His voice barely a whisper, he leaned forwards and said, "You want tea? A BLT?"

When the woman nodded, he turned back to the waitress.

"Make that two. Two teas, two BLTs"

Her pen poised over her pad the waitress said, "Are you sure?"

"I'm sure," Hanson said.

When the waitress left the woman said, "I'm Carol Jones."

"I'd never get to Heaven if I filled my head with glue... what's it all to you?" McCartney.

Carol Jones said, "What's your name?" and when Hanson told her said, "I need your help, Jay. And need is the operative word here. If I didn't need it, I wouldn't ask."

The donkey-jacket-wearing lorry driver stood. Stepped back from the counter. Frowned at Hanson as he passed but said nothing.

Not having eaten since the night before Hanson had been hungry and thirsty but now was tempted to leave before their order arrived.

'Jimmy Dean... James Dean...' David Essex.

Only he hadn't thought in terms of his order. Had thought of leaving before their order arrived.

Carol Jones said, "I can't go back alone in case Raymond's waiting."

'...she love him she love him but just for a short while...' Bowie.

Hanson closed his eyes. Opened them again. Would have sworn all the red in there seemed redder than before.

Especially the red on the left side of Carol Jones' face.

Beside him Carol Jones said, "I feel stupid."

"You shouldn't," he said. Glanced at her and saw there were tears in her eyes.

She was supposed to buy a lottery ticket but—tired and distracted— had forgotten. His anger sudden as milk boiling over on a hot stove.

"He thinks the only chance of a better life he's got is if he wins the lottery."

Hanson hoped for a big win, too. A chance to buy a house that didn't have a cellar plagued by damp. To see that Mollie got the things she deserved. Visited the places she'd always wanted to visit. A whole new life for the two of them.

"That doesn't excuse what he did."

Driving along the seafront Hanson saw nothing that would have kept his old man holed up in Barmouth all these years. The fayre minus fun, the few shops on the seafront deserted, the beach empty but for a crashed kite.

Being on the beach was what he remembered most about Barmouth.

His old man reading a western by Louis L' Amour as the waves rolled in. This the only time he ever saw his old man read. The intensity of it what stuck in his mind. The book held tight. Each new page fiercely bent back. His head pitched forwards as if intent on devouring the words.

Yet three quarters of the way through his old man had stopped reading and tossed the book down. The tortured pages curling up like the legs of a dying insect.

Later, he'd tossed the book into a bin.

When Carol Jones said, "Are you alright?" Hanson realised the Polo was practically at a standstill because he'd been searching the sea front for bins. If he'd seen one was ready to pull over and rummage through it. Hoping to find a long-abandoned copy of *The Quick and the Dead*.

Thinking such a fucking stupid thing annoyed him!

Also annoying was the fact that it wasn't true to say the beach in Barmouth was the only time he ever saw his old man read.

For a time in the early Seventies every Monday evening the three of them had gathered round to watch *Alias Smith & Jones* and when the show finished his old man always read the credits. Why? Maybe that was something else he'd ask him when they caught up. His list of questions growing all the time.

Perhaps some of the annoyance Hanson felt found its way onto his face. Trepidation in Carol Jones' voice when she directed him to turn first left and then hard right into Brook Crescent and park directly outside a three-storey house.

Hanson shut off the engine. Carol Jones breaking the silence when she said, "At first Raymond made me feel wanted." Laughed bitterly and said, "I know what that makes me."

Hanson was about to reassure her that that wasn't the case until he remembered Mollie telling him that sometimes it was better to say nothing. Better just to listen.

"The second time we went out I couldn't get my breath. Raymond said I needed to see his GP." She nodded. "I switched GPs and when, three or four-months later, Raymond said we should move in together it seemed the right thing to do."

She leaned forwards to better facilitate her view. "We rent the top floor," she said. "Not we," she amended. "Not anymore."

Carol Jones led the way along a shortish hallway and up three flights of dusty stairs.

Facing a heavy oak door at the top of the third flight of stairs, she hesitated.

Here to help her if the need arose, Hanson wondered if he was up to it. His old man had promised that when he was old enough, he'd teach him to look after himself. Which he took to mean he'd teach him to fight the way he and his Uncle Kevin could fight.

Except they couldn't.

Deciding he wanted to take on the Legion's Treasurer after failing to kick his wife to death Kevin had felt the need for back up.

Maybe that was when his old man's nose had been broken. His uncle and his old man together not able to drop the Treasurer. Fighting not their thing.

Besides which his old man hadn't delivered on his promise anyway. Left him and his mother before he deemed him old enough to teach him to look after himself.

Carol Jones unlocked the door. Pushed it all the way open. The tension in her shoulders apparent. Her footsteps brittle-sounding on the threadbare carpet.

Hanson saw the ceilings were high. The furniture faded.

What looked like confusion on her face Carol Jones said, "None of this is mine."

With him by her side she crossed the living room to another heavy oak door.

Light lay across an unmade bed. Reflected off matching wardrobes and bed-side tables.

Carol Jones strode to the nearest wardrobe and opened it. From it took a tan-coloured suitcase and said, "If he got to keep my passport it'd feel like..."

She slid her passport into a manilla folder packed with papers and placed it in her suitcase, then quickly added a few clothes. Left the rest swinging morosely back and forth and crossed to another door.

Hanson glimpsed a drip-studded shower curtain and blue ceramic tiles.

Seconds later Carol Jones emerged carrying a toothbrush and toothpaste, shampoo and conditioner and face cream. All of which she zipped into her suitcase.

"It's light," she said, testing its weight. Grinned as if she'd heard a good joke, though alarm registered on her face when she heard the outer door to the apartment slam shut.

Nobody wanted dealings with Pete Hodgetts. He was big but that wasn't why —there were bigger kids at Bristnall Hall Secondary School.

Partly, Hanson put it down to reputation. Stories of Hodgetts always in circulation. How he took on the Whitehouse twins when he was in the first year and they were in the fifth year and they came off worse. How one day a gang from another school were waiting for him and rather than run away he charged them. Punching, kicking, biting.

And partly, he put it down to Hodgetts' dead eyes.

He had no intention of ever appearing on Hodgetts' radar but that wasn't how it worked out.

"You're the cunt put one past our Eddie," Hodgetts said. Eddie Hodgetts' younger brother. Would-be goalkeeper in the second-year football team.

Standing by the bike sheds, Hanson hadn't ever scored a goal in his life and was about to say so when Hodgetts drove an elbow into his face before he could speak. An explosion inside his head what it felt like. Didn't remember hitting the ground. Did remember using his arms to try and push himself upright as Eddie meandered over.

"That's not Craig Brown," Eddie said.

"Cunt shouldn't look like him, then," Hodgetts said as he strode away.

Sometimes, when he felt how he'd felt when Hodgetts floored him Hanson dreamed of lashing out. Like Caine in *Kung Fu* his fighting skills beyond compare. Too fast, too strong, too skilled to be overcome.

"When you can take the pebble from my hand..."

But dreams were all they were. He'd never lashed out and had no fighting skills to speak of. Why hearing the outer door to Carol Jones' apartment slam, he felt his stomach clench.

Was he a match for Raymond Decker? The answer was almost certainly no. But if it came to it, he'd do what he could to stop him hitting Carol Jones again. Was by her side when—moving quietly—she stepped out of the bedroom and into the living room—

Seeing the outside door shut, just her and Hanson in the living room Carol Jones said, "Wind must have blown it closed." Relief in her voice.

Standing on the landing a minute later she put down her suitcase and took out two keys. Placed both on the floor inside the apartment, then straightened up and turned to look at Hanson.

If he was supposed to say something he didn't know what it was. Settled for watching her close the door without further hesitation. The click a terse reminder that there was no going back.

An ice cream van passed by. Hanson so relieved to be outside it was tempting to stop it. Buy them both a 99.

Instead, he unlocked the Polo. Watched Carol Jones put her suitcase on the back seat and get in. Got in beside her and fed the key into the ignition.

"Where to?" he said. Trying to lighten things by sounding like a taxi driver.

Expected to be directed somewhere nearby. Surprised when she said, "Llandudno."

Llandudno was the holiday with his parents Hanson remembered most. Had been twelve going on thirteen the summer of '74.

In his head whole chunks of the lyrics and all the tunes of: 'Jealous Mind': Alvin Stardust, Terry Jacks: 'Seasons in the Sun', The Rubettes: 'Sugar Baby Love'. 'When Will I See You Again?' The Three Degrees, 'Sad Sweet Dreamer': Sweet Sensation.

Lately, more and more often lyrics and tunes came unbidden. Sometimes wrestling him from sleep.

'Sad sweet dreamer, it's just one of those things you put down to experience...'

He'd heard them on the radio. Seen them performed on *Top of the Pops*. Had felt left out if he didn't watch *Top of the Pops* even though they didn't have a colour TV. Jump suits and flamboyant flares rendered only in black and white.

The Triumph Herald was gone by then. Replaced by a green Ford Escort. Did it have a radio? Seatbelts? Had he still taken a comic book to read on the journey? Hanson had no idea. Didn't remember any of the journey there, though he did remember the three of them being in Llandudno. Its Victorian pier. A tram to the top of the Great Orme.

Had they taken the tram? Of course not. His old man saying it was stupid to spend money when they had legs to walk on. His mother maybe saying something in reply, maybe not.

Hanson remembered their ascent of the Great Orme as the one sunny day of their holiday.

From the top they'd seen the sea spread like a vast blanket. Shielding his eyes from the glare of the sun Hanson had tracked the progress of an oil tanker across the horizon. Wished he were on it. Heading anywhere.

'But the hills that we climbed were just seasons out of time...' Terry Jacks.

His mother wore a light summer dress, his old man wore a short-sleeved cheesecloth shirt, Hanson's sun-burned neck hurt.

Hanson opened his mouth—

Ready to tell Carol Jones that—strangely, or curiously, whichever was the right word—he'd intended to search for his old man in Llandudno, but the cost of a new exhaust and lack of sleep had caused him to change his plans and he intended to go home today. Back to his wife, Mollie. Though he'd drop her somewhere, of course. A coach or train station, perhaps.

But closed it when Carol Jones pushed her tongue over her dry lips and said, "There's nobody in Barmouth I can stay with."

'...when will I share precious moments?'

She said until yesterday she'd attributed her lack of friends to her work at the ice cream parlour. The work exhausting despite that the owner often told her when they didn't have a queue of customers it was okay to work steadily.

Carol Jones told Hanson how Dennis caught her taking screws from the base of the automatic ice cream maker, wiping them off with a cloth, then reinserting them. Felt driven to be busy, busy, busy.

"Raymond was our best customer. Always bought himself a sundae but hardly ever touched it. Kept looking over at Dennis..."

She shook her head and said, "I have a sister who lives in Llandudno." Then as if she'd read his mind said, "Raymond might be waiting for me at the coach or train station." Her eyes on his cassette tapes - '72, '73 or '74 scrawled onto each of the spines—she said, "Raymond's a copper."

Taking the A470 because it was the quickest route Hanson said, "Llandudno was one of the seaside towns where I planned to look for-" and stopped.

But it was already too late.

"Look for?"

Traffic was light. The sky overcast. He hoped a bout of silence would extinguish her question, but it didn't.

Carol Jones said, "I told you things I haven't told anyone else."

Hanson held out for as long as he could. His voice cracking when he said, "I'm looking for my old man," and told her how not long after they got back from Llandudno, he came home from school to find his mother standing in the tiny kitchenette with red eyes.

When she told him, she didn't take him in her arms and hold him. Never good at such things, she sat him at the kitchen table and prepared a huge meal for the two of them.

After eating some of it, they sat looking everywhere except at each other whilst half listening to the radio until darkness closed in around them.

'Sad, sweet dreamer, it's just one of those things you put down to experience...' Sweet Sensation.

"I haven't seen him for twenty-five years," Hanson said.

'Sad, sweet dreamer, it's just one of those things you put down to experience...'

As fine drizzle continued to fall, he said, "My mother sang along to the radio. Would get the words wrong and laugh."

Her laugh was something that always lifted him. Something he spoke at length about until in a voice that sounded far away Carol Jones said, "Why are you trying to catch up with him now? After all this time?"

They were close to Llandudno when Hanson pulled over at another café.

In for a penny, in for a pound, he thought.

This one with a row of tall conifers bowed by the wind behind it and a nearly full skip in front of it. Old chairs and broken tables piled high in the skip. The drizzle on hold but the promise of more in the air as he eased into a space and turned off the engine.

The place was newly refurbished. The smell of new furniture stronger than the smell of food.

'You could be out with him... And I would never mind... Ah-ha-ah-ha it's just my jealous mind...' Alvin Stardust.

Carol Jones didn't want anything this time around.

Hanson's mug of tea was brought to a window booth by a bearded man who smiled at him and said, "Anybody ever tell you that you look like Steve Buscemi? Or am I thinking of Tim Roth?"

Hanson smiled. When the bearded man left—with Carol Jones beside him—remembered the opening of *Alias Smith & Jones*. The two outlaws on the run from the law. Horses galloping, shots fired. Hannibal Heyes saying: *"Kid, there's one thing we've got to get."* Kid Curry saying: *"What's that?"* With the sound of more shots fired Heyes saying: *"Out of this business!"*

Turning, Hanson saw the *McVities Family Favourites* tin on the seat next to him. Must have carried it in without thinking about it.

His tea still too hot to drink he removed the lid and picked out three photos of his old man.

"Tenby in '72, Barmouth in '73, Llandudno in '74."

He spread them on the table for Carol Jones to see. No indication of what she was thinking from the expression on her face.

When her scrutiny ended, he put the photos back in the tin.

Realising it for the first time only as he spoke Hanson said, "When I'm in supermarkets I see faces that remind me of him."

It'd got so he moved tentatively along the aisles.

Just a few days ago the likeness was so marked he'd abandoned the trolley with his shopping and walked out empty handed.

Carol Jones said, "When we get to Llandudno, I'll help you look for him."

It was mid-afternoon when they got there and parked on a street a few minutes' walk from the seafront. Carol Jones pointing at one of the houses opposite and saying her sister lived there.

"Is it OK to leave my suitcase in your car while we look for your dad?"

"Of course."

Hanson picked up the *McVities Family Favourites* tin. With fumbling hands opened it and shuffled through the photos. Their colours eye-achingly bright even beneath the overcast sky.

"My old man used to say he wanted to be a Bingo caller," he said.

Put the photos back in the tin and placed it on the back seat next to Carol Jones' suitcase.

The colours in there were almost as bright as his photos and the sound of a pinball machine seemed to have penetrated his skull as with Carol Jones beside him, he wandered up and down the narrow aisles. The place smaller than he remembered it if back in '74 they'd stepped into this arcade.

Had they?

As if desperately searching for an answer Hanson studied the faces of the few people in here.

None of them looked remotely like his old man had looked in '74 or what he imagined him to look like now.

Sweating heavily, he was about to suggest that they get out of there when Carol Jones said, "We can ask there," and pointed at a glass booth near the back.

Hanson said, "Bingo."

The man in the booth raised his eyebrows.

"I'm looking for the Bingo caller," Hanson amended.

Wearing a Cure tour tee-shirt, the man in the booth said, "We don't do Bingo, haven't got a Bingo caller."

Sweat running stingingly into his eyes Hanson was tempted to ask if they had once upon a time, but let it go.

'Will I have to wait forever? Will I have to suffer?' The Three Degrees.

The wind dragged sweat from his face as they trudged along the seafront to the pier. His hands deep in his pockets. Tiredness weighing ever more heavily on him.

'Sad sweet dreamer...' Sweet Sensation.

There were no customers in any of the shops on the pier. All the shop-keepers detached looking.

But was it any fucking surprise this early in the year?

'Sugar baby love...' The Rubettes.

Hanson tried to imagine his old man working in one of the pier arcades as a Bingo caller.

Couldn't do it but with Carol Jones by his side felt obligated to press on. Saw how the manager of the first arcade stared from her booth as if she were a waxwork exhibit.

"Make the same mistakes..."

Without even stepping past the threshold, he saw there were no Bingo boards and headed towards the second arcade.

It was run by an old man.

But not his old man.

And again, there were no Bingo boards.

Hanson slogged away from the second of the pier's arcades.

'It's just one of those things you put down to experience.' Sweet Sensation.

Nodded when Carol Jones said, "We could go to the top of the Great Orme."

Side by side they walked away from the summit station to where the Orme offered a view of all Llandudno. The blue-grey sea rolling in against the curve of the beach. The pier pointing like the long hand of a clock. Tall houses along the seafront. Parked cars before the tall houses—a seemingly endless line of them, though not his old man's old Polo.

'And every time that I was down...' Sweet Sensation.

Not...

'You would always come around...'

...his old man's?

Stomach knotted with tension, without turning from the view Hanson said, "Are there any bookshops in Llandudno?"

Carol Jones said, "I think there's a *Waterstones*, but I'd need to ask my sister to be sure."

His eyes on a seagull hanging on the wind Hanson said, "Sometimes I buy books."

'Sad sweet dreamer...'

In his mind he saw a small pile on his bedside table and said, "I start reading, but, somehow, I don't ever get around to finishing them." Heard Carol Jones laugh at that and say it was something she did, too.

At least Hanson thought he heard her say that.

But when he turned to look at her, Carol Jones wasn't there.

It was dark but Hanson didn't switch on any lights.

'Metal guru is it you? All alone without a telephone...' T Rex.

He placed the *McVities Family Favourites* biscuit tin and his holdall exactly where he'd picked them up from two days ago.

Was it only two days ago?

He waited a moment without knowing what he was waiting for.

'I said mama we'er all crazy now...' Slade.

It was after midnight. The house silent. The smell of damp stronger than when he'd left it.

'But I ain't forgettin' that you were once mine...' Rod Stewart.

Hanson went through to the kitchen. By moonlight watched as if hypnotised as a tear plopped from the tap.

'Oh, soley soley...' Middle of the Road.

Was it Mollie who hadn't turned the tap off fully?

Was it?

'How can I be sure... Where I stand with you?' David Cassidy.

He poured himself a glass of water and drank it down in one. The biting cold a comfort to his throat but torture to the backs of his tired eyes.

On the drive back from Llandudno he'd been forced to pull into a layby. Slept for a while and when he woke followed the beams from his headlights all the way home.

Hanson rinsed out the empty glass. Upended it on the draining board and shivered.

'Sad, sweet dreamer...' Sweet Sensation.

Careful to make no noise he climbed the stairs.

Gathering himself he paused outside their bedroom door, then pushed it open.

'...it's just one of those things you put down to experience...'

Through the dark saw a small pile of books on his bedside table.

To Tame a Land, The Burning Hills, Hondo, Sackett, Comstock Lode —all Louis L'Amour westerns.

'Sad sweet dreamer...'

No sign of Mollie.

The bed not slept in.

At first, he'd thought it was a joke. Thought maybe, despite everything that had recently happened to her, Carol Jones had tasked herself with cheering him up because that's what he looked in need of.

A joke to cheer him up, yes.

So—savaged by winds sent to assault the Great Orme and scowled at by tangled grey clouds moving fast in a south-westerly direction—he'd searched for her. Hurrying towards where-ever she could conceivably have got to in the seconds since she said, "*I think there's a Waterstones, but I'd need to ask my sister to be sure.*"

But after many frantic minutes of search—when there was no sign of Carol Jones—sweating again and breathless, Hanson had stopped. Stood still. His mind racing as seagulls screamed above him.

What the fuck was going on?

Hanson had thought of Mollie by his side, always by his side, then buried that thought.

'*Been another blue day without you girl...*' Sweet Sensation.

Temples pounding, he'd hurried to the summit station. Stood next to an old man with a black and white dog. The old man thin. His cheeks gaunt. What was left of his white hair dancing in the wind.

It was a slim chance he knew, but could this be not just any old man but his old man?

Fuck no! Hanson knew it couldn't be. Knew it! No uncertainty about it—fucking knew it!

"He likes you," the old man had said.

Hanson had tried to smile but couldn't. Was relieved when the tram arrived.

Descending from the Orme it had occurred to him that Carol Jones was part of some scam.

But what the fuck was there to scam from him?

No money to speak of. The house not paid for.

'*He's outrageous...*' Bowie.

The Polo worth next to nothing because his old man hadn't taken care of it!

His old man hadn't...?

'*...He screams, and he bawls...*'

What?

The Polo was worth next to nothing was what the mechanic at *HiQ* had told him. Higgs... That's right, he told himself.

It was worth next to nothing, but even so Hanson wouldn't have been surprised to see it gone.

But the Polo was exactly where he'd left it. Nothing changed except Carol Jones' suitcase was no longer on the back seat.

Had he mis-remembered?

Had her suitcase been put into the boot?

Hanson checked.

Nothing in there except a near-bald spare tyre and a rusted scissor-jack.

Slamming the boot closed harder than was necessary he'd reeled around; sure he'd see someone was watching him. This all an elaborate hoax. A joke at his expense.

But no one was watching him.

It occurred to him that Carol Jones had got to the Polo ahead of him, had somehow taken her suitcase from the back seat, so he strode over to the house she'd said belonged to her sister and rang the doorbell. Clearly a man in a hurry was about to ring it again when the door opened.

White-haired and stoop-shouldered, the woman was surely way too old to be Carol Jones' sister and still Hanson had asked.

"I don't have a sister," the old woman had insisted. Warily watched him retreat to the Polo.

'In a world that's constantly changing...' David Cassidy.

He'd retreated to the Polo, yes.

But not to the Polo, no.

To *his old man's* Polo, yes.

In a daze he'd got in and driven off.

His old man's Polo...

His old man's...

The unfamiliarity of the house was chilling.

'You were always on my mind... You were always on my mind...' Elvis.

Starting to shake, he drew back the curtains and sat on the edge of the bed.

'Keep thinking about you girl... All night long...' Sweet Sensation.

When he turned, Hanson knew he'd see Carol Jones seated on the opposite side of the bed though she wasn't there, hadn't ever been there.

'...Been another blue day without you girl...'

Carol Jones said, "You know," and Hanson nodded. Couldn't hide from it anymore.

"Yes."

'...been thinking about you girl...'

Tomorrow would have been their anniversary, but Mollie had died two years ago.

"Two years..."

'Was so happy when I found you...'

A cerebral haemorrhage.

'But how was I to know... That you would leave me walking down that road...'

No warning until she complained of a severe headache.

The weight of it bore down on him. Looking at his hands he recalled that his old man died not long after Mollie, leaving him the Polo.

Gathering himself, Hanson stood. Blinked. In the past two years had made it to Tenby a couple of times, Barmouth once, but never to Llandudno before. Reached down to straighten the bed where he'd sat and whispered her name, "Mollie..." Then again.

Wasteland

Where was his drink? Palmer was pretty sure he hadn't finished it though he felt like he'd drunk it and half a dozen more, and in a big fucking hurry!

So loud he'd have sworn it made his teeth vibrate, the music also had something to do with the way his head felt and was what drove him to ask Allenby if the parties he threw ever gave him a headache.

Allenby grinned. "What'd be the point having ten grand's worth of sound system if they didn't?" The boss man pushed his tongue around inside his mouth as if to clear away something he'd been chewing. "An' as for my neighbours, which was going be your next question... fuck 'em!"

It hadn't been his next question. Palmer didn't have a next question. But he didn't say so. Instead, knowing Allenby expected as much he laughed at what the boss man had said.

"What's the point havin' money if you can't say fuck the neighbours?" Allenby demanded. Palmer ready to oblige with more laughter when the boss man's expression suddenly changed.

This sudden change of expression was one of the boss man's favourite tricks. Something gauged to cause maximum discomfort in whoever was facing him. But it was something Palmer had grown used to which was why, his laughter checked but still on hand should it be needed, he was able to wait. Didn't say anything and resisted the urge to go grab another drink—fuck searching for the old—and the impulse to escape despite that he believed he'd be better off anywhere but here or his new flat.

"What's that you're wearing?"

This wasn't what Palmer had expected. But then delivering unexpected comments was another of Allenby's favourite tricks.

"A Ted Baker Tailored-Fit," Palmer said. Touched the lapel of his jacket with his fingertips as if to confirm it.

Allenby made a meal of laughing. Pushed out his reddened cheeks and rocked back and forth on his wide hips.

Palmer felt as if Allenby's music had penetrated his skull. As if the rapid, pounding bass had aligned itself to his heartbeat. What the fuck was this shit he was playing anyway? Palmer had listened to music his whole life, but none of what he'd heard tonight was familiar! How the fuck could that be?

Turning left then right to show how his jacket moved without losing its shape Allenby said, "This little beauty set me back only... three grand!"

"You're kiddin' me?!"

"Nope!"

Palmer had been kidding. The boss man's suit three grand's worth of ugly as far as he was concerned. That Allenby hadn't twigged, something to hold onto when a new tune erupted from the speakers. The pounding bass more rapid and urgent than anything that had gone before and his heartbeat immediately and sickeningly as one with it.

"I feel bad about what happened with you an'..." Feigning concentration Allenby narrowed his eyes and waited.

Again, Palmer thought about grabbing the nearest glass. Gulping it down then getting out of there. But he didn't. Thought of what it would cost him and said, "...Lauren."

"That's it!" His face relaxed again. And as if he was keeping score Allenby held up a finger, though of what he was keeping score only he knew and he wasn't telling. "I feel bad about what happened with you an' Lauren so I'm gonna' speak to my tailor an' tell him when you come to see him, he's got to treat you right!"

Palmer fought back the desire to tell the boss man not to fucking bother. A fight he might have lost if at that precise moment Allenby hadn't said that here was someone he just had to meet.

As if in answer to a question the woman gazed directly at Palmer and said, "I wanted to be a flapper...Like from the Twenties!"

Before stepping briskly away, Allenby winked at Palmer.

Looking at the woman with the bobbed blonde hair and Twenties-style gold silk dress Palmer wondered what the fuck Allenby's wink meant. He was sure the pounding bass was keeping him from clear thought. Would've sworn the bass line had sped up still more and got even fucking louder. Like his heartbeat. Shit, his heart trying to hammer its way out of his fucking chest! Was it possible to have a heart attack at thirty-one? Palmer imagined himself clutching his chest and pitching violently forwards. Crashing into the woman with the bobbed blonde hair and careening off her before hitting the floor deadweight, stone cold dead. If it happened that way, he was certain none of the rich bastards at Allenby's party would bat a fucking eye. Would just carry on sipping wine and chatting.

"You think I look like a flapper?"

Even in two-inch heels the blonde woman was half a head shorter than Palmer, slim and blue-eyed, smiled up at him.

"Glenn said I should talk to you."

Palmer wanted to ask her what else Allenby had said and a whole lot fucking more, but before he could she leaned so close he was able to smell her perfume. Something familiar that made goose bumps rise.

The blonde woman said, "What made me want to be a flapper was seeing *The Great Gatsby*. The movie with Leonardo DiCaprio, y' know?"

Distracted, Palmer searched the room for a mirror. Suddenly needed to know if he looked red in the face and ready to keel over from a heart attack or premiership sharp. Until Allenby's comment, in his pale grey *Ted Baker*

Tailored-Fit and black *Moss Bros* shirt with matching tie he'd thought the latter. Now, he wasn't so sure.

Unable to locate a mirror Palmer said, "Right!" Told himself that if you were in doubt 'right' was always the appropriate thing to say. Disagreement for losers and fools.

"Has anybody ever told you that you look like Leonardo DiCaprio."

The flapper smiled.

Palmer didn't. Beads of sweat popping out on his forehead and his shirt glued to the base of his spine, he studied the flapper's teeth. Small, white, and even.

"Glenn said you were nice."

To avoid pressing her on what other lies Allenby had told her about him Palmer focused on counting how many were with them in the lounge. He made it eight. Didn't know any of the eight rich bastards in here with him and the flapper and was glad of it, though the fact that he couldn't locate Allenby was un-settling! Where the fuck was the boss man? Hiding out somewhere? Watching him from his hiding place?

Palmer told himself to stop being fucking stupid! But if he was just being stupid, why, with only ten people in a lounge this size, did the place feel so fucking crowded it was hard to draw breath?

"Sorry!"

He focused on the flapper again. Looking directly at him she seemed to be waiting for something. Palmer had learned that if you didn't opt to say 'right' or nod you had to smile if you wanted to get on in life. Disagreement for losers and fools. Why he smiled at the flapper when he said, "What're you sorry for?"

"Did I introduce myself?"

"I don't think so," Palmer said. Recalling how Allenby had winked at him he tried to ignore the burning dryness at the back of his throat.

"I do that sometimes," she said. "Forget to introduce myself, I mean."

"Alright," Palmer said. Threw in a nod for good measure. He wondered if Allenby would be put out if he made some excuse and moved away. Or if to offend the flapper was to offend Allenby too? Felt as if he was being watched. His skin crawling.

"You should grow a beard," the flapper said.

Nodding smoothly at what the flapper had said Palmer re-counted. Still there were just ten of them in there and no sign of Allenby. It meant the boss man was hiding. Fucking had to be! Palmer pressed the back of his hand against his top lip. Knew it was fucked up to think that the boss man was watching him but couldn't help it.

"I'm Connie."

The flapper held out her hand and Palmer shook it. Her slender fingers so cool to his touch he was tempted to press them against his forehead.

"Glenn didn't tell me your name."

Connie raised her eyebrows, but Palmer failed to notice. Couldn't shake the feeling that Allenby was spying on him. The fat fuck studying his every move. Some sort of test underway and the stakes sure to be high!

"You're supposed to tell me who you are, now," Connie prompted. Stood directly before him with the fake pearls at her throat reflecting shards of light from the crystal-finish pendant directly above them.

"*And* Palmer," Palmer said, and wondered, when Connie repeated it with the emphasis on 'And' just as he'd known she would, if he'd told her *And* Palmer was his name because something about her reminded him of Bree-Anna.

Palmer inspected the brown leather shoes he'd polished that morning then faced Erskine. Who cleared his throat and said, "What you're seeing here's in excess of 10,000 square feet of warehouse."

"Alright," Palmer said. Nodded and smiled smoothly.

In his late fifties, twenty pounds overweight and balding, Erskine said, "You're not a pushy prick an' I like that. Allenby an' the others he sent were like wolves. Here."

Palmer accepted a mint. Popped it into his mouth and sucked on it as thirty feet above them a pigeon swooped from the rafters.

Erskine said, "Promised my daughter I'd live longer." Mimed lighting up a cigarette and blowing out smoke, closing his eyes when the nicotine hit. "Now I don't smoke but look." He opened his jacket to show Palmer the way his gut bulged over his trousers.

His attention on the frantic beating of the pigeon's wings—somewhere high above and to his right—Palmer nodded.

"If I'd shown my gut to Allenby or those other pricks he sent, they'd have said I wasn't fat, just big-boned!" Erskine patted his stomach as if it were a dog, then led them over to the entrance where, grunting with the effort, he yanked open a steel door.

Outside it was overcast, the promise of rain in the air. Palmer took in the idling truck opposite them, saw the driver glance over at Erskine for the thumbs up then roar away, exhaust fumes billowing.

As if absorbing the silence left by the truck, for a full minute Erskine was still. Then, running his fingers through what remained of his hair he turned to Palmer and said, "In the old days there'd be twenty trucks out here." He popped another mint into his mouth. "Someday I'm gonna' be the boss here, it's never in doubt, but my old man tells me I need to understand the men who work for me so from when I'm ten years old, seven days a week after school I load trucks, thought my old man was full of shit but was scared to say so, knew if I did he'd kick my skinny arse!" Erskine grinned. "Hard to imagine now, but in those days, I did have a skinny arse!" He sucked hard at his mint. "Anyway, fact is I did it the way my old man said I should. Worked from the bottom up an' in forty years never had any workforce problems!"

Looking out at the expanse of empty yard fronted by railings, some of which were twisted and some of which were broken, and at litter sent spiralling by gusting winds Palmer nodded.

"But a year ago I knew this place had to be sold." Erskine passed a hand over his jaw. "That was when Allenby came knocking. First him, then, when I sent him packing with his tail between his legs, the pricks he sent in his place."

Winds cutting at him, conscious of the cracks in the concrete beneath his feet and the weeds gathered at the base of the warehouse, Palmer followed Erskine across the yard. Was so cold he was ready to call it a day and get out of there. Prepared to tell Allenby that he'd pushed Erskine like he'd told him to, but Erskine wasn't interested in selling until Erskine tossed another mint into his mouth and said, "I could've got more a year ago than I'm gonna' let you have it for today."

Standing before the oak desk in Allenby's top floor office an hour later Palmer said, "I just did it the way you told me."

Made entirely of hardened glass the west facing wall afforded a view of tower blocks and clogged arterial roads, a supermarket, and a bronze effigy of a long dead local luminary.

Allenby usually avoided eye contact. Preferred to gaze out at the Five Ways. At maddened traffic and hurrying shoppers. But today, with his forearms braced on his desk and his fingers tightly laced together, the boss man brought his narrowed eyes to bear on Palmer and said, "Tell me what happened... Slowly!"

Erskine crossed the yard to the railings and gripped them as if they were the bars of a cell. Blood draining from his fluorescent-tube-fingers he said, "You're not a pushy prick like the others he sent an' I like that, but it's not why I waited so long."

Palmer's eyes drifted over to his Polo. Parked a quarter of a mile from Erskine's warehouse, it had seen better days. The paintwork scratched and the windscreen wipers so ragged that if the rain that was promised delivered Palmer would be in trouble. But he wasn't concerned. Believed he'd be able to get rid of the Polo because Allenby provided company cars for the men who negotiated successfully. Picturing himself at the wheel of one of the black 4X4s Allenby Developments dished out Palmer almost grinned. Had to work hard not to. Had to work hard to keep nodding at what Erskine was saying. Erskine in need of a fresh fucking mint when he released the railings and let his arms fall to his sides.

"Knowing none of the men who worked for me won't be able to afford the houses that'll be built here's why I waited so long, but now..."

Looking Allenby in the eye Palmer smiled and said, "I kept pushing him the way you said I should."

Holding the contract Erskine had signed flat on his desk as if it might otherwise be snatched away from him Allenby stared at it.

"I offered the minty prick more than this a year ago!"

Allenby's tone prompted Palmer to wonder if he'd have to keep the Polo after all. If he did it was time to get new wipers fitted and maybe take it to a valet service.

But Allenby sounded more relaxed when a moment later he said, "You're married, yes?"

"Yes."

"Laura!"

"Lauren."

"Lauren, that's right!" Grinning now, Allenby said, "I want you to ring Lauren an' tell her you'll be late home because we're gonna celebrate your first deal for Allenby Developments!"

Two hours after he made the call to Lauren the woman raised her eyebrows and said, "I've never met anyone named *And* Palmer before."

Hearing the woman who called herself Bree-Anna say this after three bottles of Stella on an empty stomach Palmer almost choked.

Dark-haired and dark-eyed, wearing stilettos, black latex bra and pants, Bree-Anna tilted her head to one side. "Are you laughing at me, *And* Palmer?"

They were upstairs in one of the private booths. Palmer on a Boutique Upholstered Chaise Longue. Bree-Anna standing before him, the lighting low.

When he had himself under control Palmer reached for his wallet, but Bree-Anna shook her head.

"I'll dance for you."

What he wanted was to touch her bare shoulder, the skin there lightly and evenly tanned.

Only it wasn't. It turned out it was Bree-Anna's natural colour. The south of Italy where she'd grown up. English not her first language. How Allenby managed to confuse her when he told her she was to take Palmer up to one of the private booths and dance for a man who was so great at cutting deals he might one day make partner.

In which case it'd be, "Allenby *and* Palmer Developments."

That she wasn't tanned wasn't the only thing Palmer got wrong about Bree-Anna that night.

Later, in a freshly painted kitchen she told him she was, "Just Anna!" Saw from his face he was disappointed but shrugged and said, "You're not And Palmer, I'm not Bree-Anna, an' guess what? Allenby's not who he says he is either!"

The sky was filled with stars, the pavement was coated with frost, and although Palmer hadn't grabbed another drink before they left Allenby's party, he still felt drunk. His head spinning and the houses opposite dipping and weaving away from him.

Telling himself the cold air would help he drew in deep breaths. But the cold air didn't help! If anything, he felt fucking worse!

"Are you okay?"

Palmer saw the blonde woman beside him wore a thick coat that was almost to her ankles and still she looked frozen. He was sure she'd told him her name, but it shifted away from him like the houses opposite! "This's insane!"

"What?"

The blonde woman had been smiling. Now concern tightened her face.

It was insane that he'd had very little to drink and still felt fucking drunk and that he couldn't bring to mind the name of the woman looking expectantly up into his face, though Palmer was sure neither of those was what he'd meant when he said it.

So, what the fuck had he meant? Palmer looked into the woman's blue eyes and said, "Nothing."

Wondering if he'd convinced her that this was so, he threw in a smile.

Trying not to look as if she was watching him carefully the woman held her collar tight against her throat.

Pretty sure that he hadn't convinced her of anything Palmer let the smile fall from his face. "Look at his fuckin' house!" Frowning, he muttered, "Who the fuck's Allenby?" But if the woman, whoever she was, heard his question she gave no outward sign. Following his directive, she simply turned to face the house they'd just a few moments before hurried out of without saying goodbye to anyone.

"See?" Palmer demanded. Recalled as his gaze skipped from the house that they'd just left to another much like it how the man who called himself Allenby had told him that any of the properties in Castle Close would sell for at least—

"Connie!"

Relieved that the name of the flapper had come to him Palmer grinned. Maybe he wasn't losing his mind after all!

"Yes?"

Palmer said, "What d' you think these properties are worth?"

Connie gave his question careful consideration. "A lot," she managed finally.

There was sufficient moonlight for Palmer to pick out freckles on Connie's cheeks. He hadn't noticed them before. Put at ease by them he said, "How d' you come to know Allenby?"

"I'm cold," Connie said. Shivered to emphasise what she'd said.

"It is cold," Palmer agreed. Turned to her and said, "But how d' you come to know Allenby?"

"You said you'd take me home!"

It sounded like an accusation.

"Is that your car?"

Every week Palmer used to take it to be cleaned and afterwards would admire the way the paintwork shone when light hit it but didn't anymore.

"What're you doing, *And* Palmer?"

Palmer seemed as surprised as Connie to see his wallet was in his hand.

"Cash," he said, and showed her the dozen twenties he'd drawn from an ATM earlier that evening.

Her eyes seemed huge. This, like her freckles, something else he hadn't noticed till they were outside. Was it possible that out here in the cold her eyes had become bigger? Palmer told himself to stop being stupid. Jammed his wallet back into his pocket and hurried over to his 4X4—parked near the entrance to Castle Close like a getaway car.

"This's a great car," Connie said when they were inside with the heater on full.

Four of the dozen or so cars parked in Castle Close were Allenby Developments purchases identical to the one in which they sat, yet Connie had picked out his without hesitation. Palmer studied her. Here in the cab couldn't see her freckles anymore. "How d' you know this one was my car?"

Her face in shadow, Connie seemed suddenly fascinated by the way the frosted pavements reflected sodium light.

Palmer turned off the heater and waited.

Made uncomfortable by the silence and the way his hands gripped the wheel as if it were something he was trying to squeeze the life from Connie said, "Don't be angry with me, *And* Palmer!" Then, as he turned to face her, ready to tell her not to call him 'And Palmer', not now, not ever again, she said, "In this light you look even more like him."

"Leonardo DiCaprio," Palmer said despite himself. His head spinning faster. Everything before him dipping and weaving more violently than before.

It was Saturday fucking night so why were the roads so quiet. Not even Uber cunts zipping past? Was everybody at home, safe and sound, watching TV? Or had half the world disappeared? What a fucking thought—but when Connie asked him a second time if he was okay Palmer said, "I'm good."

She placed her hand lightly on his thigh. "Turn here."

When Palmer cut the engine and got out of the 4X4 he became aware of the stink from the bus stop by the entrance to the car park.

Following Palmer's gaze Connie said, "A man was murdered at the bus stop last night or the night before." She told him nobody in any of the apartments had seen or heard anything and when the forensics team were finished cleaners arrived and sprayed everything with disinfectant, when she was done giggled and said, "I know!"

Why was she giggling and what the fuck did she know? Before Palmer could ask, Connie took his arm in hers and led him over to Kenelm Court. There, speaking quickly, she told him climbing the stairs was part of her exercise routine. Her fitness instructor who had taught her how to clench her glutes with each upward step.

Palmer thought he recalled Allenby recently mentioning a fitness instructor and like his tailor, Allenby's fitness instructor came with a strong recommendation.

"Max says if you have a firm butt, you'll have a long life," Connie said as she climbed: step-clench-step-clench. Told him Max had done everything from hardcore bodybuilding to ironman events. Said, "Max is the man!"

Unable to remember if Max was the name of Allenby's instructor, Palmer repeated: "Max is the man!"

Pretending not to notice Connie said, "Here we are."

She didn't put on a light, but even in near darkness it was clear to him that the place was way bigger than Bree-Anna's.

Holding himself still he tried to imagine what it would be like to stretch out on Connie's couch. Unable to do so Palmer pressed his thumb against his temple as if to dig out the pain there. The pounding that had come on at Allenby's party undiminished.

Registering Palmer's hesitancy Connie said, "Check out the view!" Placed one hand firmly against the small of his back and with the other pointed out first the motorway—a brightly lit curve describing the horizon—then the park over the road from Kenelm Court: tall trees rearing up through the darkness. She said that although you couldn't see it from her flat, between the M5 and the park was a canal and a stretch of what had been industrial land, what was now wasteland.

It'd be necessary to open a file on Connie pretty soon! That she mustn't call him 'And Palmer' would go in there. As would that she wasn't to direct him to look out of the fucking window. But for now, Palmer let it pass. "Alright," he said despite that he was focused on the flats to his left not what Connie pointing out to him. The flats visible only when he leaned so close to the glass that his own face was reflected at him. Grey smudges beneath his eyes and his cheeks sunken.

The furthest of the three flats was where Bree-Anna lived.

Maybe that was why the pounding in his head seemed to be getting worse! Lauren had always encouraged him to carry codeine, though he didn't have any with him now. Knew he could ask Connie if she had any, but instead backed away from her and the window with his gaze lowered.

"Damian?"

Palmer froze. Against the backdrop of the darkness outside he saw that the sheen of Connie's gold-coloured dress was more pronounced. Saw too that she was trembling and tried to recall details of the movie she'd mentioned when Allenby brought her over to him but couldn't. Nothing clear to him.

"I'll get you a drink."

When the pounding inside his head moved up another notch Palmer bit the inside of his cheeks. A trick he'd learned as a boy.

Swallowing blood he said, "Connie?" Paused then said, "I didn't tell you my name was Damian!"

Outside, Palmer braced his hands against his knees as if he'd been running, though he believed—minus the step-clench—he'd walked not run down from Connie's apartment.

He looked over at the bus stop. Remembering what Connie had told him, he shivered. Empty except for the driver the last bus rattled past without slowing. After which it was quiet.

Connie had looked disappointed when he walked out.

Palmer shook his head. No, that wasn't it. She'd looked as if she'd let someone down. Who? He straightened up and took out his wallet. Maybe Connie was watching from the window she'd directed him to look out of. He hoped she was but didn't turn to see. Tossed away his wallet then got into the 4X4. Sick of being told what to do ignored the electronic voice that urged him to put on his seatbelt and exited the car park at speed.

Back when he only knew her as Bree-Anna her irritation at his laughter, if irritation was what it was, vanished when Palmer said, "I'm not laughing at you, I promise!"

Bree-Anna sat beside him. Her face turned expectantly towards him. "Why don't you want me to dance for you?"

Palmer said, "Tell me what Allenby said." When she had he explained what he'd meant and assured her that he wanted her to call him 'And Palmer' anyway. Told her beyond that what he really wanted wasn't for her to dance for him. Rather he wanted to touch her bare shoulder. Knowing it was company policy for customers to look not touch he was sure Bree-Anna would refuse but she didn't.

Her skin felt even smoother than it looked and ten minutes later in faded blue jeans, a white blouse and a pair of flat-heeled shoes Bree-Anna took his hand in hers and led him down three flights of back stairs and through the staff kitchen.

Wondering if she'd changed out of her latex underwear Palmer followed her out of a fire exit into the night air. Saw the stars were glittering pin pricks and the buildings opposite them were silent but watchful. When the fire door closed crisply behind them thought he heard Bree-Anna say, "There's no going back now, *And* Palmer."

Moving quickly, she led him along a narrow alleyway between tall buildings to the Five Ways. Where streetlights cast a sickly glow over the leafless trees fringing the road, the entrance to the underpass, and a nearby road sign to which was bound two bouquets of lilies—one that was old and dry, the other that was fresh and clean.

Palmer liked that, holding his hand tightly, Bree-Anna was hurrying. But why was she? Was it the *Ted Baker* Tailored-Fit she liked the look of? Or the brown leather Jasper Conran shoes—the first pair of actual shoes not trainers he'd owned since leaving school?

Having decided now was the time to see what the 4X4 was capable of Palmer drove ferociously from Kenelm Court. It helped that the glistening roads were empty—Saturday night turned into Sunday morning. Was he headed home?

Gnawing at the inside of his cheeks to draw fresh blood, Palmer knew he wasn't. The flat where the things he'd taken from the house still sat in two Dickins and Jones suitcases someplace he'd never call home!

In fact, Palmer was headed in the opposite direction to his new flat. The park Connie had pointed out to his right and the tall trees forming its border hiding the stars from him. Was it their towering intention to intimidate him? Sure, it was, but he wouldn't have it, yelled, "Fuck you!" and punched down the accelerator. Speeding from the threat of the trees turned hard right and saw the wasteland was separated from the road by slatted gravel-board panels.

Snapping his attention from the fresh lilies Bree-Anna said, "Where's your car, *And* Palmer?"

Allenby had driven him to the club. Remembering this was the case Palmer pushed the fingers of his free hand across his forehead as if to peel off something glued to his skin. Should he ring Allenby and let him know that he'd left Gentlemen Only? He knew it was the decent thing to do, but when Bree-Anna kissed him all thoughts of the boss man vanished in an instant.

"I've had too much to drink to drive," Palmer said when Bree-Anna drew back from the kiss. He expected she'd return to the club to find someone who could drive her home. Allenby maybe! A part of him even wished that she would, but that wasn't what happened.

"We'll get a taxi," Bree-Anna said and led them to the side of the road. Still teeming with traffic though the rush hour had ended hours ago.

Palmer was disoriented when he woke the next day. Knew only that it was still dark, that his mouth tasted bad, and that he wasn't alone.

From outside he heard the hydraulic whine of a refuse collection van. He was naked and the weight of Bree-Anna's head on his shoulder had numbed his arm. Though he tried to disentangle himself without waking her, she stirred immediately.

"I have to go."

"I'll make you coffee," Bree-Anna said and seemed to move from under the duvet and into a satin robe in a single fluid movement.

Palmer knew if he left immediately there'd be time to collect his car and still catch Lauren before she set off for work. He'd tell her how he got Erskine to sign, Allenby's insistence on taking him out to celebrate, and the promise of a black 4X4. He'd tell her they drank too much, and he'd spent the night on Allenby's sofa. Pulling a face to show Lauren the pain he was in. Felt sick at the thought of lying to Lauren until Bree-Anna smiled at him with her small, white, even teeth.

Five minutes later they were in her kitchen. The paper on the walls faded with age. Lit by a single bulb Bree-Anna turned from making coffee and said, "Tell me, Mr Property Development Man: what should I do to improve this place?"

Remembering how Bree-Anna had laughed at the look on his face when he saw she still had on her latex underwear, until she turned and spoke Palmer had been about to press his lips gently to her neck. The coffee-coloured skin there smooth and taut. But now, faced by her question he almost blurted that he knew fuck all about property development. Acquiring Erskine's warehouse had been blind luck. Working for Allenby Developments the same with maybe a twist of opportunism thrown in...

He'd heard that applying to Allenby Developments was worth a punt even with no experience if he had a connection to the military since Allenby had trained at Sandhurst! Palmer had never even been a boy scout. Nonetheless, looking him in the eye he'd told Allenby he'd been in 45 Commando and had been deployed in Afghanistan. The first time the unit had been used since the Falklands conflict. Impressed, the boss man said, "Welcome aboard,

Lance-Corporal Palmer!"

Standing in Bree-Anna's kitchen, for the first time Palmer wondered why Allenby hadn't ever checked out what he'd said and found him out to be a bare-faced liar!

What if he, Mr Property Development Man, could get hold of the wasteland to his left? Palmer knew if he could Allenby would be happier even than when he'd told him he'd got Erskine to sign on the dotted line. Happy Allenby a sight to behold. A fortune in dentistry on display and relish in the rich-bastard eyes! But wouldn't it be far better if he could cut out the boss man altogether?

"Fuck Allenby Developments!" Palmer yelled as the spiked railings and slatted gravel-board panels blurred by, as the tyres of the 4X4 crunched grit and, taking the piss he was sure, a full moon grinned down at him. "Bring on Palmer Developments!"

Palmer pictured himself in Allenby's office. The boss man staring out of the window at the Five Ways until what he was saying about the new deal and the new company he'd formed hit home.

When it did Allenby's face would twist with anger. Enjoying the boss man's outrage Palmer would tell Allenby he had a few things to get straight. Starting with that he should shove the 4X4! He'd toss the keys onto the boss man's desk and say he had no use for it, planned to get something sportier!

Was that all? No, he'd tell Allenby he'd decided to stick with *Ted Baker* Tailored-Fits because unlike the overpriced pieces of shit he wore they were cool, and maybe when he said it, he'd execute a little turn as Allenby had at his party, rubbing salt in the wound by showing how a suit hangs when your hips aren't wider than your fucking shoulders!

Was that all? Palmer shook his head. No, he'd spell out that the services of Allenby's personal trainer were something he could do without even if the guy was the one Connie had raved about—a bodybuilding martial-artist who could fart wonders and shit miracles!

Was that enough? No, Palmer still didn't think so. Decided that his parting shot would be to tell Allenby he'd never been in the military and didn't understand why the fuck a former Sandhurst man hadn't checked him out and exposed his lie. After which he'd mock-salute and show him a clean pair of heels!

The scene would play very, very sweetly, he believed. Why in spite of the resolute pounding in his head and the taste of blood on his tongue Palmer was grinning. His grin fixed firmly in place until he struck the kerb—

Face down Palmer watched Connie dancing to a pounding bassline emanating from deep inside his skull. Her silk dress, fake pearls and bobbed blonde hair whipping back and forth as the tempo increased.

He intended to ask her who the fuck had told her to wear the same perfume as Lauren when he saw her lips were snapping open and closed like scissors, and heard her say, "You're bleeding, *And* Palmer!"

At which point, panicked, he used his arms to push himself upright.

Blood was smeared above the right eye of the face staring at him from the rear-view mirror. Palmer recognised the face as his own, probed the blood-smear with his fingertips and saw beneath it a quarter inch long gash. Further probing established that the gash was wide but not deep, after which he turned dismissively from his reflection and saw that though the airbags hadn't been deployed the 4X4 had mounted the pavement and come to rest at a forty-degree angle to the road.

Something on the dashboard was pinging in time to the frantic bass-line Connie had been dancing to until he turned off the ignition, opened the door and let cold air rush in.

Memories of the dancing flapper quickly dissipated as he got out, pocketed the keys, and shut the door.

Beyond the wasteland he heard the M5. It said it loved him, though Palmer knew it was lying.

The pounding in his head hadn't let up. Fed by the love song of the motorway it seemed intent on wearing him down, crushing the life out of him!

But he wouldn't let it, said, "Fuck you!" and stepped over to the near-side of the 4X4.

A quick inspection revealed there was no damage to the bodywork, just a burr on the outside of the front tyre. Squatting a yard from the gravel-board panels Palmer let his hand rest against the rubber, which was surprisingly cool to the touch.

Three yards from the 4X4 he located a half house brick. It, too, felt cool to the touch. Cakemore Road was like an empty river with the park on one side and the wasteland on the other. Apart from the song of the motorway, the riverbank was quiet, what was left of the world sleeping off Saturday night. That was good! Holding the half house brick tightly in both hands Palmer smashed it against the nearside wing, the passenger door, and the rear panel above the fuel cap, when he was done stepped back to inspect his handiwork.

Satisfied with what he'd achieved he tossed the half house brick at one of the gravel-board panels and dusted off his hands. Made up his mind that once Palmer Developments was established, he'd for fucking sure get himself something sportier than the 4X4.

Enervated by his decision Palmer strode to the nearest of the panels, boosted himself up and sat astride it. He laughed out loud, didn't know why, told himself it didn't matter, from where he sat the song of the motorway louder, the expanse of wasteland bigger, what looked like a whole fucking world down there in the darkness.

Sodium light from the motorway exit strip illuminated a stretch of canal not visible from Cakemore Road or the window of Connie's flat. The M5 was a spoiler, no doubt about it, but canal-side properties were desirable! A cold wind slashed at his face then raced across the wasteland, cowing long grass and nettles. There was a killing to be made here. He could go start his research right away. On the laptop at his new flat find who owned the wasteland and any previous offers, any likely legal difficulties. But the thought of unpacked suitcases and virgin saucepans drove him to lower himself down onto the wasteland and, as frost-coated grass soaked his Jasper Conran shoes, whisper, "No going back now, *And* Palmer."

Seeing Bree-Anna got to be a habit then much more than that. "With you I feel different," Palmer thought he remembered telling her the second time he went to her apartment. Bree-Anna with her arms around him. Dressed to the nines as if she'd known he was coming.

Grass and nettles clutched at his ankles, the uneven terrain made his thighs tremble, and to top it all his head was still pounding. Palmer wondered if he really had told Bree-Anna that with her he felt 'different'.

Breathing hard he paused to get his bearings and saw he'd moved just twenty yards from the gravel board panels when it felt as if he'd walked for hours and was close to being lost. He told himself to push away such thoughts but couldn't, his fingers cold, his lips dry.

The second time he saw her Bree-Anna said, "I didn't leave the club with anyone before, And Palmer. I've had offers, believe me, but I turned them all down, understand?"

Conscious of the heat of her body Palmer bit back the desire to ask her why with so many offers she'd elected to leave with him. Knew even though the *Ted Baker* Tailored-Fit and Jasper Conran shoes did look pretty fucking cool that didn't account for it!

His trajectory illuminated by sodium overspill from the motorway Palmer set off again. Tried to walk faster but couldn't, the grass and nettles waist high in places and hungry for him.

The canal drew him towards it, but when he was halfway there, he paused again. Knew that industries had long since been banned from dumping waste yet would have sworn that he could smell beneath the rank stench of rot a fresh ammonia tang.

Wrinkling his nose, he passed a hand over his face as if to wipe away something foul, and remembering Lauren's advice about leaving wounds to heal resisted the temptation to use his fingernails to rake open the newly formed scab above his eye.

Turning away from the canal Palmer saw that he was now a hundred and fifty yards from the gravel-board panels and that without him being aware of it the land had dipped so sharply the panels formed a horizon beyond which it was no longer possible to see the trees surrounding the park.

It shocked him. The shock what drove him to button his jacket and set off again.

After a dozen more yards the decline became sharper still. As if he was walking on ice how he felt. His thighs fibrillating. His breathing a series of sharp gasps. It wasn't right that he should be breathing so fucking hard! He decided that when money from Palmer Developments was rolling in, he'd get himself a personal trainer after all. Not Max the man but someone with a similar pedigree who'd get him into top shape. Palmer pretty sure that he'd always secretly wanted to be an athlete.

His mouth filled by the taste of blood Palmer stopped to rest again. Bent forwards at the waist with his hands on his knees he assured himself that when money was rolling in and he'd got himself a big house and a sound system capable of pissing off his neighbours and a sporty car he'd make acquiring a bodybuilding-martial-artist-personal-trainer a priority. Didn't want to end up like Allenby—old before his time!

His lungs burning, Palmer wondered how old Allenby was. Didn't know. Whereas the boss man knew his age, that his marriage was over and, if Bree-Anna had spoken to him as he suspected was the case, a whole lot fucking more!

Still breathing hard, but suddenly infuriated Palmer straightened up and spat, though the taste of blood remained. As part of his drive to get into shape he'd need top of the range tracksuit and trainers, but not *Adidas*, he decided!

Palmer remembered how on a zero-hours contract at *JD Sports*, decked out in *Adidas* sweatpants, tee-shirt, and trainers, in the run up to Christmas with the store operating extended hours and long queues at every available check out Sanders was always offering him more work: yet another long shift.

Like all the bosses he'd ever worked for Sanders was tall. And like all the other *JD* employees he wore *Adidas* kit, advertising the products they sold something that was 'essential' Sanders said, 'essential' one of his favourite words.

It came back to him how Sanders would brief them before the start of every shift. Settled an *Adidas* baseball cap onto his head, called them into a huddle as if he was their coach, they his team and told them it was 'essential' to maximise sales and perform optimally. According to Sanders everything was 'essential', but especially appearance, why once he stopped mid pep-talk and pointed at the scuff marks on the trainers of another of the zero-hours guys.

"So what?" the guy said. Something Sanders repeated. Turned the words over in his mouth the way Erskine turned over mints in his. After which, his message crystal clear, they didn't see the guy with the scuff marks on his trainers again despite that in the run up to Christmas they could have used him.

To Palmer on the other hand, newly *Adidas*-outfitted and desperate to work after lengthy bouts of unemployment punctuated by compulsory Job Seeker courses in how to compose a CV Sanders was all smiles.

It made Palmer want to laugh but he resisted. Needed the money so badly he kept smiling back at Sanders until the first Saturday in February when, with frost on roofs and the sky washed out looking, he turned up and saw there was no smile to return.

"What's wrong, Top?"

Did Sanders see himself as *Top Dog* or *Top Gun*? Palmer had no idea. He knew only that Sanders' Monika was something else he'd always wanted to laugh at and hadn't. Not being greeted by Sanders' smile why he spoke without thinking, though he still believed his question couldn't be as damaging as the question asked by the guy with the scuff on his trainers.

Looking as if someone had taken a dump in his baseball cap Sanders said, "Did I ask you to come in today, Palmer?"

Wishing that he'd been the someone who took a dump in the big man's baseball cap Palmer said, "I—"

But Sanders held up his hand as if to stop traffic. "You don't just show up here! It's essential that you wait for me to call you. Essential that you wait for me to tell you there's work here for you!" Trying to look as if he was genuinely hurt by the lack of understanding Sanders said, "I thought you knew that was how we did things here, Palmer!"

For weeks Palmer had bottled up his laughter. But now as he faced Sanders in the area where staff were corralled each morning for their team talk found that he couldn't any longer.

Tears ran from his eyes and rolled down his cheeks.

When all his bottled-up laughter had gone Palmer said, "You said 'we'! But I don't see any 'we', Top. I just see me an' you. Me standing here like a spare dick an' you talking to me as if I'm a piece of fuckin' shit!" then let Sanders walk him out of the store with the other employees watching closely whilst pretending not to.

Palmer decided that when he was getting into shape he'd wear Ron Hill as his first choice of sportswear, Nike as his second choice. Decided that if push came to shove, he'd wear any brand of sportswear except fucking *Adidas*, though the key was that come what may he wouldn't ever again be escorted off premises!

Above the thundering rush of two trucks chasing one another along the motorway Palmer shook his head. Didn't intend ever to be shown the door again, though when he'd apologised to Allenby for leaving Gentleman Only without him had expected the boss man to be pissed off.

Only Allenby had grinned and winked.

Palmer put the boss man being easy on him down to luck. That first night with darkness wrapped around them like a blanket had said to Bree-Anna, "You're my lucky mascot." Or had he? Pushing through clinging grass he told himself it didn't matter. The important thing was that for a time he'd convinced himself it was true. An idea that was reinforced by what happened next.

Informed of the new deal he'd brought in, Allenby had come from behind his desk and said, "What's the secret of your success?"

There was a brief lull in traffic, a sudden quietening that coincided with Palmer reaching the canal and standing on the flagstones. He was sure that the lull meant something, just not what. Following it a convoy of coaches roared by each so close to the one in front it was as if they were a single creature.

When the creature was gone Palmer focused on his more immediate surroundings. Pierced by reeds, the dark water reflected haloes of orange light, whilst across the way rubble had been packed around the motorway stanchions. Spiked railings circled the stanchions. Who the fuck did they have to be protected from? Never mind, he told himself. Unzipped and peed into the canal. The arc of urine fracturing the haloes and setting off ripples.

He shook off and zipped up, in answer to Allenby's question hadn't said that Bree-Anna was his lucky mascot, instead had said, "I do things the way you told me!" Did saying that make him a suck up? It did, but maybe he could be excused because it wasn't true.

Erskine rang him the day after he'd signed the contract. Said to meet him, named a place and hung up.

Palmer didn't remember giving Erskine his number, but having spent the night with Bree-Anna wasn't thinking straight enough to feel unnerved by it. Far more pressing was that he felt hung-over, which was odd because ordinarily even on an empty stomach he was able to take four or five bottles of Stella in his stride.

Feeling way too rough to park the Polo out of sight and hike, Palmer parked directly over the road from the café where he'd arranged to meet Erskine, shut off the engine and looked out the window.

The sky was grey and still he was so hung-over the light hurt his fucking eyes! Squinting, he lowered his gaze and focused on the café. Why had Erskine picked such a shithole for them to meet? Paint peeling off the exterior woodwork and the sign so grubby all he could make out was the letter O. Nor was it just the café. There were potholes in the road and the newsagent's next door was boarded up as if it'd been under siege. The whole area a fucking eye sore. Despite which Palmer straightened his tie as he crossed the road.

Seated at a table near the smeary front window but not looking out, immediately Palmer entered the cafe Erskine said, "I used to come here all the time," and with his fluorescent tube fingers gestured for Palmer to sit opposite him.

Their table had on it a freshly laundered, blue-checked tablecloth with a fresh pink carnation in a ceramic pot as a centrepiece.

The carnation was a nice touch, but Palmer's mind was elsewhere. Feeling more hung-over by the minute, he sat. Had Erskine caved to sentimentality and changed his mind about the sale? Decided he wanted to keep his warehouse after all, his memories if nothing else stored there? Palmer geared himself up to tell the old man a contract had been signed and there could be no going back. But before he could Erskine swallowed what was left of one of his mints and said, "This place's still called Olivia's but Olivia's dead."

Palmer said nothing. Keeping still he tried to recall what Bree-Anna had whispered when he was inside her.

When Erskine said, "I knew her," Palmer's chest tightened. He tried to swallow but couldn't and shook as adrenaline coursed through his hung-over body.

But Erskine hadn't somehow read his mind. Wasn't talking about Bree-Anna. Cleared his throat of minty mucus and said, "Olivia was my wife's friend, a classy lady," then turned to the man behind the counter, the man's dark hair scraped back into a ponytail, pointed first at the empty cup before him then at Palmer.

Looking at Palmer intently, Erskine said, "Olivia died the same day as my wife, you think that means anything?"

"I don't know," Palmer admitted. Too tired to do otherwise. The other tables in Olivia's empty, but the stink of fried breakfast pervasive. He felt hungry and sick, both. Had Erskine already wolfed down a full-English?

Erskine said, "I don't know either." His hand gripped by tremors took an un-opened tube of mints from his pocket and placed them on the table.

The dark-haired man placed cups of tea before them then returned to the counter to pore over a newspaper.

Erskine lowered his voice and said, "Olivia's son. He's the same age as my daughter."

Was Erskine about to ask him if that meant anything? Palmer tried to get an answer ready in case, but thoughts of Bree-Anna kept getting in the way, crowding him.

"They're both about the same age as you," Erskine said. Spooned sugar into his tea and stirred.

Palmer shifted in his seat, the pain in his head worse and the smell of friend food stronger. Surely there was someone else in Olivia's, shovelling down breakfast? But, turning, he saw he'd been right first time: he and Erskine were the only customers.

Having decided to call Bree-Anna, so far as he knew no plan in mind other than that, Palmer was about to get up and leave without explanation when Erskine gulped tea and said, "I didn't get you here to talk about any of that."

Walking and talking quickly, Mercer said, "Jimmy rings me an' says you're a decent kid, if I'm looking to make a deal with no shittin' about, I should talk to you, so here we are."

Where they were was a biscuit factory near the front of the trading estate off Bromford Lane, a quarter of a mile or so to their left a train station, a few hundred yards to their right a van selling burgers with patio furniture set out before it.

Palmer stood next to Mercer, facing a padlocked iron gate. Mercer sixty and deeply tanned. It was early afternoon. Mercer unlocked the gate and led them in.

"You like biscuits?" Mercer grinned. Accentuated by his tan, his teeth were dazzlingly white.

Palmer hadn't eaten anything all day, the sickness he'd felt in Olivia's now become something else.

His hangover, too, seemed to have become something more. Was he feverish? Certainly, he was overly warm and felt as if his thoughts had been speeded up, become difficult to hold onto. Was Mercer offering him a biscuit? Should he accept?

Leading Palmer across a short strip of tarmac to his factory Mercer said, "Everybody likes biscuits. You make biscuits, sell them at the right price an' you'll never lose money."

It seemed he was being offered advice and, his throat too constricted to speak, Palmer responded by nodding.

"Two offices and a reception area, everything else shop floor or loading." Mercer led them into the nearest of the two offices and said, "It'll take one phone call, couple of day's tops, an' the whole place'll be clean as a whistle." Mercer whistled. Registering that Palmer didn't smile he said, "Don't look so serious."

"I..."

"Don't worry about it." Mercer sat at a cluttered desk and indicated that Palmer should sit opposite him. "This's how it used to be when I interviewed. Only not many of the people I ever interviewed wore a *Ted Baker!*"

Palmer wondered if he should smile. Before he could Mercer said, "I know just one unit's not what you're after, Jimmy put me in the picture."

What fucking picture? Palmer blinked. Erskine had made a phone call from Olivia's with only a fresh pink carnation separating them and still he had trouble grasping what was going on—including reconciling himself to the fact that the Jimmy of whom Mercer spoke was James William Erskine.

Mercer said, "I own four more units on this estate," and whistled again.

The whistle reminded Palmer of cartoons he'd watched as kid. A whistling sound what was used when a character plunged from a great height. Was that what was happening here? Was he falling from a great height? At any moment would he hit the ground? Only instead of flattening out like a cartoon character then getting up again, his fucking head would explode, splattering blood and bone everywhere!

Mercer laughed and said, "Not four more biscuit factories! I mean everybody likes biscuits, but not five factories worth on one fuckin' estate!"

Palmer wanted to ease from the chair to the floor and lie with his eyes closed, breathing deeply until he could think straight. If he did how would Mercer react? Palmer judged it best not to find out.

Mercer said, "The other four units are empty." When Palmer still didn't say anything, he nodded approvingly. "Jimmy said you knew how to fuckin' listen."

What? Palmer felt like a fighter between rounds, the advice of his corner men bouncing off him.

Mercer took a folded sheet from his pocket and pushed it across the desk.

Palmer didn't know what Bree-Anna meant to him. He knew only that he'd rung her when he stepped out of Olivia's. Leaving James William Erskine to tackle what may well have been his second full-English of the day.

Picking up on the third ring Bree-Anna said, "I'm glad you rang, And Palmer," that he believed her the only light in an otherwise dull day.

"What's on there you didn't get from me," Mercer said.

Palmer reached over and opened the sheet. Saw the names of five individuals besides which were phone numbers and figures grouped into columns indicating gross annual income set against expenditure.

Mercer said, "It's as plain as the nose on your face three are losing money hand over fist an' the other two aren't making enough for it to matter." As if he'd just performed a magic trick Mercer held his arms out to his sides. He said, "I'm moving out of manufacturing an' into investments." Pushed out his lower lip then said, "Jimmy said you were a decent kid so I'm bringing this business your way." Mercer took a second folded sheet from his jacket pocket and pushed it across the desk towards Palmer. "That's the price for my units."

Palmer glanced at the second sheet. He had arranged to go back to

Bree-Anna's flat and was wondering if she'd be naked when he arrived.

Erskine had connected him to Mercer and the Polo with the ragged windscreen wipers had been consigned to history before the end of the week.

Palmer frowned. Maybe that made Erskine the secret of his success? Or had he really stumbled on a lucky mascot after all and everything that'd happened was down to Bree-Anna?

Palmer stumbled and almost fell. In stumbling wrenched his lower back and grimaced, pressed his right hand firmly against the source of the pain and held himself still, when he did so saw that he was fifty yards from where he'd taken a piss with no memory of having pushed doggedly through more clinging grass and nettles.

The canal was to his left, the motorway beyond it. Its love song unchanged. Disingenuous but reassuring.

Pressing hard against the screaming muscle Palmer reminded himself that he was here to scope the wasteland. Planned to acquire it for his business. Everything he'd ever wanted just a few moves away.

Consoled by thoughts of his success he wondered if the stars still hated him. He was pretty sure that they did, but not why and, refusing to ask, focused on the storage container yard abutting the wasteland.

A quarter of a mile or so ahead, picked out by perimeter nightlights he saw the containers were piled high and told himself that was good. It meant that he didn't have a view of the flat he used to share with Lauren way back fucking when!

Palmer noted that the gravel-board horizon to his right seemed further away than anyone could walk no matter the credentials of their personal trainer or the quality of the *Ron Hill* sportswear they wore and as the pain in his lower back eased rediscovered the pounding in his head.

The pounding had slowed, but clearly had no intention of letting up. "Alright," he said, and using the tips of his fingers broke open the scab above his eye, the new pain sharp as first light.

Lying naked on her bed the second time he visited her flat—the planes of their bodies defined by early evening light—Bree-Anna turned to face him and said, "You're married, but not happily."

On a floor below them a radio played a familiar tune and waiting for her to continue Palmer tried vainly to recall the title of the song.

"If you were, you wouldn't be here," she said.

As one familiar tune gave way to another, he watched shadows shift stealthily across the ceiling.

Bree-Anna said, "Don't be sad, *And* Palmer."

Was he sad? Was that why he was with Bree-Anna?

He had met Lauren during an induction day at the New Street branch of *Costa*.

A twat if ever he saw one, from the moment he set eyes on the branch manager Palmer was dubious of his ability to survive the day.

Stating the obvious, the branch manager said, "I'm the branch manager." Easily six foot two inches tall Greenwich said, "You can call me Mr Greenwich unless a customer asks to see the branch manager, in which case you must refer to me as: 'the branch manager.'"

Palmer considered saying something but since he had just £3.85 in his pocket checked the impulse.

Greenwich faced four seated would-be recruits, all of them wearing plain black trousers and *Costa* tee-shirts. They were at the rear of the premises in a space Greenwich insisted was a training room, though Palmer noted a mop and bucket leant against the wall behind them.

Holding a permanent marker Greenwich moved to stand before a flip chart, unlike the would-be recruits wore a shirt and a tie.

Palmer pressed his fingers against his temples, but it didn't help. Sitting there felt like being back at school and it was hard not to stare fixedly out the window.

Greenwich said, "With the person next to you, one being a *Costa* employee the other a customer and then swapping, I'd like you to role-play that scenario," plucked the cap from the end of his permanent marker with relish and added, "We'll feedback in a few minutes."

The pair to Greenwich's left threw themselves into their role-play as if they'd been waiting their whole lives for such an opportunity.

Meanwhile, Palmer turned, and seeing that the woman next to him didn't think much of this either whispered, "What scenario?"

On the flip chart Greenwich wrote COMMITMENT and SERVICE. Underlined them both then furrowed his brow.

When the woman looked Palmer in the eye he wondered if she was able to see into him. All his thoughts laid out like items of bric-a-brac at a car boot sale.

If she was able to, for once he didn't mind.

She said, "I'm Lauren."

If she was able to see into him, wouldn't she already know his name? Certain that she would, Palmer told her anyway.

When Lauren stood, Palmer stood too, and followed her to the corner of the training room where the mop and bucket were stowed.

She whispered, "The scenario's what Greenwich just said." Seeing he still looked blank she explained.

Greenwich wrote ACHEIVEMENT on the flipchart. Underlined it three times then added an exclamation mark and stood back to inspect his work.

When Lauren began her role-play, Palmer bit the insides of his cheeks. It didn't help.

Alerted by Palmer's laughter Greenwich turned sharply from the flip chart. Conscious of the branch manager's gaze Lauren tried again. Avoiding Palmer's eyes so she wouldn't laugh herself she said, "Good morning, sir, how can I help you?"

This time Palmer managed to keep a straight face, but for only a second.

The other two recruits turned and saw Palmer bent forwards at the waist and Lauren half turned away from him with one hand pressed to her mouth, trying hard not to, but also laughing whilst Greenwich furrowed his brow again.

Palmer stepped out of the shadow cast by a branch of Lloyd's Bank as Lauren emerged from Costa, a nearby busker sang, and pigeons lined window ledges high above. He told himself that if Lauren didn't see him or saw him but didn't immediately come over to him, he'd walk away and that'd be the end of it, whatever 'it' was.

When she saw Palmer, Lauren made her way directly to him.

He said, "Fancy a coffee?" and she smiled. Beneath her denim jacket Palmer saw she still had on her *Costa* tee-shirt, only now it had a nameplate pinned to it, was glad that he hadn't fucked things up for her as well.

"Before Greenwich told you to leave? When you couldn't stop laughing an' he said it was 'non-professional behaviour'?"

Palmer fiddled with the zipper of his jacket.

Lauren waited.

"I was gonna' say: Not if you're a comedian!"

As the busker began a new song Lauren said, "So why didn't you?"

"I wanted the job." Palmer shook his head. "No, not wanted: needed."

Lauren nodded. "So?"

"What next?"

She nodded again.

"Ask you if you want to come for a drink. Not coffee."

"I meant..."

They both smiled.

After which Palmer said, "Now I've fucked it with *Costa* you mean?"

She nodded.

He considered telling her that he liked Saab 900s and planned to own one, but instead shrugged and said, "Go back to the agency." Over Lauren's shoulder he glimpsed a shadowy figure that may have been Greenwich stacking chairs onto tables and wished they'd crash to the ground. Always, afterwards, he wished he'd remembered what songs the busker had played.

Palmer didn't understand how he could have missed it! Alright it was surrounded by tall grass and nearly overgrown by brambles, but still: a dozen yards ahead were the ruins of a brick structure the size of a small house, roofless, yet with the upper walls mostly intact.

He made his way around to the entrance. The door was long gone, but as if they'd been torn aside to facilitate access there were no brambles here.

He stepped inside, where the smell of the canal was stronger, and it was darker. Palmer waited for his eyes to adjust, when they had saw directly across from him were stairs leading to what remained of the second storey.

Without hesitation he crossed the room, placed a foot on the first step and pressed—testing it with his weight. Judging that the stairs were solid enough to hold him he climbed up through the darkness to what was left of the second storey—suddenly needed to see the flat where he and Lauren had once lived.

At the top Palmer stepped cautiously onto wooden floorboards. Were they safe or, having long been exposed to the elements, were they rotten? Illuminated by starlight he saw that they were badly warped and still he edged away from the stairwell.

Up here the love song of the motorway was louder. Despite which he was able to pick out the sound of wind dashing through reeds and bobbing debris. Ignoring both, Palmer stood on tiptoe.

But all he could see were stacked containers. Were the flats where he and Lauren had lived even still standing? Palmer pressed the heels of his hands against his eyes. Knew that if you pressed hard enough you saw exploding lights. Knew for a fucking fact Lauren wasn't there and still needed to see if the flats were!

Blinking away exploding lights, Palmer wedged the tips of his fingers into the narrow spaces where mortar had been. He believed that if he could get a decent purchase, he'd be able to scramble to the top and from there—if it was still standing—see the flat where he and Lauren had once lived.

But he couldn't get a decent purchase and succeeded only in scraping flesh from his fingertips and making his chest burn with frustration. Abandoning his ascent, he flattened his palms against the bricks as if in readiness to push his way through them. The veins in his throat and temples bulging.

Minutes passed. Maybe it was hours, days, months, fucking years? Pressing his forehead against the brickwork, Palmer now chose to listen to the love song of the motorway and the litany of the canal...

When he was tired of listening, brushing specs of grit from his palms he moved to the stairwell. The opening like a hungry mouth. As he descended felt as if he were being absorbed by the darkness below and was for the first time conscious of his tiredness.

Did he have a right to be tired? Intent on checking the time, when he was halfway down the stairs Palmer dug into his pocket for his phone. Had it in his hand then didn't—

"Fuck!"

Squatting at the bottom of the stairwell he saw the screen was shattered, the phone's innards broken. Shaking his head in disgust he jammed the ruined phone back into his pocket and stood. Was about to head out of there when he noticed something over in the far corner.

Why hadn't he seen it before? Suddenly alerted to the possibility that he wasn't alone, Palmer spun round.

The darkness danced away as he twitched to the frantic thud of his heartbeat.

Turning his head slowly, Palmer studied the room carefully for the first time. Painted by shards of moonlight, the ceiling was bowed, though the concrete floor was curiously clean. High on the wall to his right were a series of holes where some heavy mechanism had once been bolted into place. What had it been? He was curious but told himself it didn't matter because the fucking nest was what he should focus on!

Careful to make no noise he moved to the far corner, where blankets were coiled like snakes around a sleeping bag that was frayed at the edges, a nest what it was, no other word for it.

Closer inspection revealed bundles of clothes and a neatly stacked pile of newspapers. Palmer pressed his back teeth together so hard his jaw bulged. Why all the newspapers? Here, what the fuck difference could the outside world make to you? Because the pounding in his head was still at him, because he hadn't been able to see the flat where he and Lauren had once lived, because of a thousand other things Palmer kicked out at the newspapers. Toppling the stack and revealing the photo album.

Had the noise been heard? Furious, and ready to fight, would someone come running?

Palmer wished they would! "Come on!" he snapped, but all he heard were the motorway and the canal playing the same fucking songs!

Convinced after several minutes that he was alone after all, he bent, picked up the album and carried it over to the doorway.

Moonlight and sodium overspill from the M5 combined were just enough for him to make out the images, though not whether they were colour or black and white. Surprised by their weight, Palmer turned the pages slowly, reverently. Nice, neat, and ordered, what he saw was a family history. Images showing men with long hair and women with short skirts he judged had been taken in the early Seventies. Which drew him to study those photos more carefully. Was it possible that he was connected to some of the faces staring up at him? Of course not! What the fuck was he thinking? He was tempted to fling the photo album into the canal. Longed to hear the satisfying splash and relished the image of ripples expanding through the darkness!

But after several moments the impulse passed and, feeling empty, Palmer drew in a deep breath and worked his way through the rest of the album. The pounding in his head suddenly sharpened by the sight of a woman leaning against a Ka.

Something about the way she stood suggested that if he told her about himself, she wouldn't make fun of him. Rather she would listen carefully and would truly understand what he was saying.

This was the last photo in the album, beyond it just empty cellophane pockets.

His head spinning with thoughts about why that might be, Palmer closed the album softly and stepped back into the derelict building.

Returning to the nest he placed the album where he'd found it and was about to re-stack the newspapers.

Instead, he paused. The cacophony in his head at a crescendo. Took the photo of the woman leaning against the Ka and slid it into his inside jacket pocket.

Immediately, he considered running. Imagined himself labouring up through the long grass to the horizon of gravel-boards.

But Palmer didn't run. Forcing himself to breathe slowly and deeply, he re-stacked the newspapers then stepped back and, satisfied that the nest looked as he'd found it, walked out of there.

The night air seemed crisper than it had just a few minutes ago. Deciding that this was a good thing Palmer pushed through waist-high grass and nettles towards the container yard, tripped and almost fell, when he righted himself focused on the nearest of two elms, trembling before him in the dark, its lower limbs no more than six feet from the floor, a fucking invitation if ever there was one!

It struck him that it'd be funny if everyone he ever knew gathered below to hear him call out, "Even in a *Ted Baker* I can climb a fuckin' tree!" What would they think of such a thing? Palmer told himself that he didn't care and hoped if he told himself so enough times it'd be true, within minutes was twenty feet off the ground and so absorbed by the climb it was as if he'd never been the man who for a time had been afraid to use any ATM but the one outside the post office at the bottom of George Road.

Winds tugged at his hair and the pounding in his head eased. Maybe if he got high enough the pounding would stop altogether? Maybe if he got high enough, he'd be able to see beyond the stacked containers and know once and for all if the flat where he and Lauren once lived was still there?

Breathing hard as he pushed higher, Palmer felt free. Feeling free, he hummed tunes that were familiar to him but un-nameable and was about to smile for his own pleasure when without warning the long since damaged limb on which he was standing snapped—

Lauren didn't look like Lauren anymore and Palmer desperately wanted to tell her so. Her face looked older and harder, but that wasn't how he'd put it. Would instead say that she was working way too hard. Was a branch manager now but still, first and foremost, a victim of the workplace: the coffee shop practically her whole fucking life! Putting his hand comfortingly on her shoulder he'd tell her that *Costa* didn't deserve her. Never had and never would. So, now he was earning money enough to pay the mortgage and then some she should walk right out of there. Take some time to decide what she really wanted to do then set about doing it. How would that be?

But Lauren spoke before he could, the hardness in her face intensifying said, "Why d' you want me to know about her!"

Palmer wanted to tell the truth but wasn't sure what it was.

Watching him intently Lauren laughed, though there were tears in her eyes. "You wanted to confess, is that it?" She drew back her fist, the force of betrayal behind it.

Palmer could have blocked or sidestepped but would have let her knuckles crash into his flesh as if he really did want to confess, did want to be punished.

But Lauren didn't hit him. Instead, she let her arm sag to her side and demanded that he show her what he'd bought his, "other woman."

They stood directly outside the jewellery store where he'd bought her wedding ring. The light grainy. People rushing past.

Lauren laughed again, though this time there were no tears in her eyes. She said, "You want to lie an' say you bought it for me!"

Palmer wished she'd hit him, knocked him down, spilled his blood! But she hadn't and now, turning to face her, "You were waiting for me," was all he could manage.

Even to his own ears he sounded surprised, caught off guard, stupid. Maybe from now on he'd introduce himself as Stupid Palmer not *And* Palmer! Because he was fucking stupid, there was no doubt about it!

Even so, how had she known?

"You made it easy for me!"

"How did I?"

It was something he hadn't meant to ask. Felt his question compounded his stupidity and guilt.

Suddenly very tired Lauren said, "It's something for you to think about later."

Unsettled by the finality of that Palmer shook his head.

But, resolute, Lauren said, "At least tell me her name!"

"Everybody makes mistakes," Palmer persisted.

Prompting Lauren to laugh harder than before. A jagged, heart-breaking sound.

After which the rain came. Furious droplets that stung his cheeks and made sustaining further denial impossible.

The rain woke him as it was starting to get light. Alerting him to the fact that the M5 was angry with him now the stars were gone!

Palmer opened his eyes and sat up. Knew that the motorway's love song was a lie but missed it and was ready to plead with it to resume until several things came to him at once.

First, the conversation with Lauren outside the jeweller's had never happened. It was true he'd gone there to buy a necklace for Bree-Anna and when he stepped outside the rain came, drenching him in seconds. But Lauren wasn't waiting for him. Found out about Bree-Anna from Anna. The look on her face one that haunted him.

Second, the pounding in his head had finally stopped. A buzzing numbness that didn't impede thinking its only residue. The jury out on whether he was grateful for that or not.

Third, he remembered he'd fallen from the tree. The moment the branch on which he'd been standing suddenly snapped and space opened up below him remembered so vividly that he braced for impact. All recall of the impact itself missing, though not the pain it had left behind. An incandescent ache that reached high up his shin and deep into his foot.

Finally, Palmer saw that he lay twenty yards from the elm he'd fallen out of—and had been covered with a blanket...

With no recall of having closed them, Palmer opened his eyes again. Had he passed out or fallen asleep? He saw that it had stopped raining and the motorway told him that it was still early, whilst the canal either didn't know or didn't care what time it was. His annoyance at its perceived indifference what drove him to sit up.

The movement awakened pain on several fronts. His left ankle, the lower left side of his ribs, and his left shoulder—a hat-trick of throbbing aches. Had he hit, or been hit by something? "I fell," Palmer reminded himself and was so caught up by slow-motion replays of his fall that for several seconds he stared without expression at the old man approaching him.

"How d' you feel?"

Alarmed by the question, Palmer threw off the blanket and struggled to his feet.

His hair long and grey, his clothes mismatched and dirty, the old man advanced steadily.

"Stay where you are!" Palmer snapped.

The old man stopped and inspected his feet as if they might choose to move of their own accord. The fact that they didn't, seemed to satisfy him and when he looked up, he announced, "I'm stayin' where I am," as if it were a victory.

Bearing most of his weight on his right leg, Palmer saw how the old man's hair was tangled and his hollow cheeks were reddened by long exposure to the elements. He thought the thin face was at odds with the chunky body until he realised the old man was wearing two pullovers and a body-warmer beneath a filthy camouflage jacket that was several sizes too large. "Who, the fuck, are you?"

"Who the fuck am I?"

Palmer drew himself up to his full height and pushed out his chest. "Are you takin' the piss?"

As a mile away hydraulic brakes hissed angrily the old man reached up to touch his straggly beard. "Why would I?"

He was cold, he realised. His Ted Baker not right for the wasteland and a night of rain. Would something from Allenby's tailor have been any better? Would even an Armani Wall Street Wool have stood up? Palmer was pretty sure not, but dismissive of the questions, despite that he felt fragile demanded to know the old man's name.

"Billy."

When wind blew Billy's hair over his face, he made no move to push it away. And when another gust did it for him Palmer saw what might have been a tear sliding down one of the reddened cheeks.

"It was me moved you," Billy said.

Palmer had been all set to call Billy a fuckwit, a dumb ass, a bozo, but hearing this elected to keep his mouth shut, as if alerted by a threatening noise turned to look at the stacked containers behind him: KLINES, FISHER and HSB stencilled onto their sides in white.

After several seconds Palmer said, "Those companies? They're all Chinese owned," said it with authority though it was something Allenby had told him and according to Anna the boss man wasn't who he said he was and couldn't, therefore, be trusted.

Billy said he used to love Chinese food and Palmer wondered if he should ask why he 'used to'? He decided not to. Instead, he told the old man that he'd fallen from one of the elms, "Like a fuckin' kid!"

Nodding, Billy held out his left arm, bent at the elbow, his fingers pointing upwards, placed his right hand with two fingers outstretched and the rest held tight against his palm near his right wrist then, suddenly, moved them away and showed the outstretched fingers colliding with his forearm twice before coming to rest at a point level with his elbow.

"You saw me fall?"

Billy pointed towards the elm, but Palmer didn't turn. Was convinced that two collisions with the tree the way the old man had shown him would account for the throbbing aches in the lower left side of his ribs and left shoulder. The damage to his ankle most probably from hitting the ground—that the daddy-pain.

"I bandaged it," Billy said. Palmer registering the bandage around his ankle for the first time then looking back at Billy, who licked his lips and said, "I was a nurse in another life."

Palmer elected not to raise the issue of 'another life' as sharp winds ripped across the wasteland, a lone duck steered a wavering course along the canal and Billy used a sleeve to wipe what might have been another tear from his cheek.

"You should eat," Billy said. "I've got food."

It'd been more than a dozen hours since he ate anything, but Palmer wasn't hungry. A sense of gratitude what drove him, limping, to follow the old man back down to the building by the canal.

From the busker's repertoire Lauren identified songs by The Beatles and Bowie which prompted Palmer to ask her what other songs she knew.

"Lots of songs," she told him at a circular table beside framed photographs of famous sportsmen.

"That's impressive."

"Is it?"

Thrown by her question, Palmer sipped Stella.

Registering his unease Lauren said, "Why'd you wait for me?"

Palmer admitted it was to tell her that he wasn't a loser.

Lauren told him she hadn't thought he was a loser, Palmer said that meant something, and six months later they moved in together, staring out of the window of their ninth floor flat without speaking something they were both much given to.

Stationed at the window as a thunderstorm tore across the sky Lauren broke a lengthy silence to ask him what, if they were on a TV or radio quiz show and he was asked to describe her, he'd say.

"That you think a lot," Palmer said.

They laughed at that. Laughing together like staring out of the window something they did a lot of. Their laughter what he remembered about the move from their flat to the ex-council semi for which they'd scrimped for a year to put together a small deposit. Despite the spectre of a twenty-five-year mortgage, with Lauren the assistant-manager in a branch of Costa and Palmer still in the grip of an employment agency their laughter why the eradication of dust from a windowsill with a damp cloth in their new home felt exhilarating.

"She fell asleep in my arms." Out of the wind, with his arms wrapped tightly around his knees Palmer wasn't cold, though that didn't explain why the fuck he was telling Billy all this. He didn't think he'd ever said such things before. Listened to the M5 hating him, sucked in the stink of the canal, and worked at keeping his mind away from the hat-trick of pain that seemed determined to take him into its arms as he'd taken Lauren in his arms the night they moved into the semi on George Road.

"You were married?"

"Not then, but later," Palmer said.

The registrar had been their only witness. "No wedding day smiles, no walk down the aisle, no flowers, no wedding dress," Lauren sang and laughed.

"What's funny?"

"Ask Bruce Springsteen," she said. Liked the fact that he still didn't get it.

"I was a married man, too," Billy said, stepping over to the stack of newspapers.

She'd polished and it stank. He hated *Mr Sheen*, but kept his lips pressed tight together to stop words inadvertently escaping. It was August, heavily overcast and muggy, though they both wore thick pullovers, sat like bookends on the settee, facing the television, each with mismatched salt and pepper pots balanced on *Eat and Be Happy* trays.

Pushing aside two potatoes she said, "I weigh ten stone."

He didn't look at her. His chicken and mushroom pie cold, he ate it anyway. Tried not to think of how on their wedding day she'd weighed eight stone and how—as she snapped away with a second-hand Leica—her mother maintained she was, "Just a slip of a girl." She used to exercise. A treadmill with the rest of the junk in the garage—a horizontal tear in the belt that for an age he'd been meaning to fix and hadn't. Thinking of it, she polished that, too—*Mr Sheen* all over it!

It wasn't only the belt on the treadmill. Lots of things in the house were badly in need of TLC. The place falling to rack and ruin while he sat and let it. Was sometimes consoled by the thought that he wouldn't be able to do much even if he could muster the energy because his tools kept going missing.

She'd taken his drill, he was sure. Had sold it most probably but knew better than to frame an accusation or demand to know what she'd spent the money on. The evidence on her breath if he cared enough to get close.

Breaking into his thoughts she said if he wouldn't let her cut his hair anymore, she could ask her friend Georgia, who'd been a hairdresser before she had kids and was a good cutter of men's and women's hair, still confident with scissors or an electric trimmer though she no longer worked in a salon.

He remembered that Georgia's youngest daughter had a rare birth defect and started to say something but stopped short of saying the word daughter.

She waited for him to start again or continue. When he did neither, to break the silence she told him her mother had kept all the cards her father had ever sent her—for birthdays, Valentine's Day, for Christmas, all signed '*with love*'. Then she shovelled the potatoes she'd earlier pushed aside into her mouth.

Such a sight might have appalled him but didn't because he was focused on the television. Seemed wrapped up in a quiz show whose exactitudes eluded him despite that they'd watched it nearly every day for nine years.

He thought that even without tools the tear in the treadmill could be repaired. That he could use Gaffer tape to bind the belt as if it were a broken arm or leg. When it was done would tell her she mustn't use *Mr Sheen* anymore because the chemicals would impair the adhesive qualities of the Gaffer tape. The lie one he was sure she'd accept and a way of moving forwards. This an expression he hated and pulled a face at whenever someone at the hospital said it.

He was sure he still had a roll of Gaffer tape in one of the compartments in his tool bag. Yet when he finished eating, he put his tray on the floor in front of him and sat back.

Initially, he wasn't paying attention to the television.

Then he was. Exactly what triggered his sudden alertness unbeknownst to him.

The third item on the six o' clock news spoke of advances in DNA technology, a cold case re view and the formation of a new website cataloguing 1,100 unidentified bodies. Joseph Walker, manager of the Serious Crime Agency's UK Missing Persons Bureau, expressed shock that such a developed society could have such a large collection of unidentified people.

Walker was replaced by a DCI with a birth mark above her left eye who spoke of the exhumation of a body found nine years ago in a river. Unidentified at the time of discovery the body was buried in the churchyard of the community who found her. "As if she was one of their own," the DCI said with an approximation of real emotion on her face.

"One of their own," he repeated. And for the first time in a long time, they looked directly at each other. Each seeing in the other's eyes the certainty that this was her.

Palmer sat still as the old man spoke. But when Billy stood, and lifted the stack of newspapers and took from beneath them the photo album, he tried to get up in a hurry, found that he couldn't and fell backwards.

"Be careful," Billy said.

Trying to look as if he was following this advice, Palmer made it to his feet at the second attempt.

With two yards between them, the old man watched Palmer closely whilst holding the photo album tightly.

It had become lighter now than when he'd followed Billy in here. Allowing him to see things he'd previously missed. A tray of cup-cakes to one side of the nest. Bottled water. Sheets of paper on which were sketches of eyes and hands. Trying not to look at the eyes, Palmer said, "I'm alright."

Having heard him decline the offer of a cup-cake, Billy picked up one of the bottles of water, opened it and handed it to him.

Palmer hesitated. Then drank, surprised by his thirst and glad to wash away the taste of blood and memories.

"Here," Billy said when Palmer had finished. Took the empty bottle from him then opened the album.

Had Palmer been capable of it he'd have charged out of there.

But before he could, Billy moved to his side. The old man able to move fluently despite the ruined face and layers of clothes.

Billy said, "On our wedding day her mother said she was just a slip of a girl."

As Billy's hand shook Palmer glanced over at the doorway. Only when he judged that it was too far for him to make it did he glance at the photo. In this light was able to see that it was in colour not black and white, and showed a married couple arm in arm, the bridegroom recognisably Billy as a young man, his cheeks unblemished.

"I loved her, but we drowned with her..."

Palmer checked the distance between himself and the doorway again.

"Not knowing was what kept us together."

Palmer noticed saw the old man's hand wasn't shaking any more.

Billy said, "Which's pretty bloody stupid!?"

Palmer looked at the photo again. A 'slip of a girl' was certainly the right way to describe the woman beside Billy. Feeling the old man's eyes on him he said, "If you say so."

It seemed to satisfy Billy, who shut the album crisply and told Palmer the 'Not knowing' that had kept them together concerned their daughter, Corrine. A day before her A Level results were due, she disappeared and nine years later, not long after a news item about a newly formed website and a DCI with a birthmark above her left eye speaking to camera, the doorbell rang as they'd both somehow known it would. When DNA samples confirmed that the body found in the river was Corrine, they arranged another funeral. "Her real funeral," Billy said. Not long after which he left, taking with him nothing except the photo album and the clothes on his back. Liked to think that his wife had got someone else to repair the treadmill.

Billy said, "She deserves to be happy," Palmer pleasantly surprised when the old man placed the photo album back where he'd taken it from and sat wearily on the stack of newspapers.

Conversely when Billy said, "You were married, but you're not married now," the surprise was unpleasant—Palmer convinced that the old man's words were an accusation.

"You're wrong!" he snapped. Regretted saying so until he recognised it as an opportunity to limp over to the doorway. "I have to go," what he said when he reached it. Almost added that he had business to tend to but stopped himself in time.

Billy followed him outside, where the motorway told him it was already late afternoon.

What the fuck had happened to the day? His ability to think clearly was gone, the pounding inside his skull was back again, his ribs were too sore for him to turn when Billy said, "I didn't mean anything."

Palmer trudged away. The pain in his ankle enough to slow, but not stop him. Grass clutching at his thighs, he opened his mouth to draw in air. Conscious of the steep incline he bore left, intending to parallel the container yard till he made it to the top of the wasteland. Once he was over the gravelboard panels and back on Cakemore Road believed he'd be able to move more easily. After getting his ankle checked out at A&E planned to crack on with getting Palmer Developments up and running but had covered less than a hundred yards when Billy charged after him.

Billy had put away the album! He'd even sat down on the stack of newspapers! So how the fuck could he have known that he'd taken the photo? Palmer knew only that as sirens screamed from the motorway Billy was on him, first alongside him and then, his ruined cheeks redder than ever, directly, and resolutely in front of him.

Palmer said, "You're in my fuckin' way!"

"Give me back the photo of Corrine an' I'll move!"

Corrine? Fuck! Since the photo was of the dead daughter should he reach into his pocket and hand it over? No. It wasn't possible to hand it back as if taking it could be readily explained, easily shrugged off. Why Palmer said, "You helped me when I fell an' I'm grateful, but right now I don't know what the fuck you're on about, all I do know is you need to move out of my fuckin' way!"

Billy pushed his arms out to his sides. Intended to become a human barrier but succeeded only in transforming himself into a scarecrow. "Give it back!"

Scarecrow or no it was clear that the old man wasn't going to let it go, why Palmer said, "You think I look like Leonardo DiCaprio?" The effect of his question what he'd anticipated, the old man flummoxed—giving him time to throw a punch.

His looping right hand caught Billy on the left cheek and sent him staggering backwards, but didn't, as he'd hoped, floor him and give him time to scramble up to the gravel-board panels and over.

Rather the old man staggered... then flung himself at Palmer.

It was dark when Palmer regained consciousness. His eyes open he lay without moving. Remembered the ferocity of Billy's punches though no pain, despite which his face felt odd. Using his fingertips, he mapped out swelling below his right eye and torn lips, commemorations of the old man's determination. Sitting up awkwardly, the hat-trick of damage caused by his fall now a wailing chorus, he reached into his jacket pocket.

The photo of Corrine was gone, but before he was able to decide what he thought about it, seated with his legs straight out before him Palmer saw that he was at the top of the wasteland. Next to the gravel-board panels. The old man's message as clear as the headlights splashing up over the arc of the motorway.

When his eyes settled on the building by the canal, Palmer slowed his breathing as if he were a sniper, readying himself for a kill-shot. Was Billy inside, carefully returning the photo of his daughter, Corrine, to the album? He could be, though it was equally possible he was nearby, watching him, ready to act if his message was ignored.

Palmer made it to his feet with the chorus rising to a crescendo and forcing him to lean against a gravel-board panel till it quieted. Certain that if he chose to ignore Billy's message it wouldn't be enough next time for him to simply repeat it, Palmer placed his palms on top of the gravel-board panel and hoisted.

The muscles in his arms and thighs trembled. How could that be when only last night he'd easily boosted himself over onto the wasteland? Despite chill winds, sweat broke on his forehead. His ragged breathing a begging letter whose please he ignored, the edge of the gravel-board bit into his hands as he struggled to the top.

There, astride the panel, he paused. Monoliths in the dark, the stacked containers to his left observed him coolly. Conscious of their gaze, Palmer turned away. Saw his 4X4 and was gripped by a memory of the look on Lauren's face when she first laid eyes on it.

"Is a 4X4 what you've always wanted?"

Lauren didn't sound pleased. Was it possible even then that she knew about Bree-Anna?

He said, "It's a great car," though it wasn't a Saab 900.

That day they drove till they were far from crowds and coffee shops. Palmer able to convince himself that Lauren didn't know about Bree-Anna because he'd been careful. The way work had expanded was a help on that score. Lauren already familiar with the sound of Allenby's name. Allenby, he'd many times told her, who kept him so late. Who worked him so fucking hard!

They parked in a lay-by and with late afternoon light flickering through trees shedding bronze leaves and got out. Seeing that there was a path, Palmer pointed, and when Lauren turned to look studied her profile for traces of something otherwise hidden.

"Let's walk," she said.

Seeing nothing in her face and glad of it, Palmer followed her.

A little way from the road they stopped as if at an agreed point. Dappled shadows moved over them as Lauren looked back at the 4X4, touched his arm, and spoke, words she repeated to him the day Bree-Anna called and told her.

"I know you like new things," Lauren said. "You always have."

Palmer had been home five minutes. Hadn't seen this coming, wasn't ready for it. The house had always been small but hadn't ever seemed so until now. Lauren watched him. Waited for him to say something. He looked over at a print showing palm trees, fishing boats and a row of stucco cottages. Had he bought this print or Lauren? Because it wasn't framed it had always allowed him to imagine that it was a window, that what he saw when he looked at it was their view.

Their view!

"Do new things make you feel better?" Lauren said.

Palmer knew that he should turn from 'their view' and meet her eyes but couldn't. Instead, he could only stare at the trees, the fishing boats.

"Why'd you fuckin' do it?" he demanded of Bree-Anna hours later. Two hurriedly packed *Dickins & Jones* suitcases on the back seat of the 4X4 and his head spinning. Did he expect her to reply? Palmer wasn't sure and still he felt surprised when—seeming to look right through him—she shrugged. Was indifference all he amounted to? The kitchen smelled of fresh paint. Shiny and bright, he was sure it was what Bree-Anna had said she wanted. Certainly, it was what he'd sorted for her. Spoke to two men who worked on properties acquired by Allenby Developments then paid them. Cash in hand, no questions asked, Palmer a man who could do deals with anybody these days, he believed.

With no expression on her face, Bree-Anna removed the necklace he'd bought her and placed it next to an unwashed cereal bowl and a stained coffee cup. "Did you think because you bought me a necklace an' had my kitchen decorated I wouldn't?"

Palmer felt as if he was being choked. Loosening his tie didn't help, nor did that it was hot in there, Bree-Anna someone who always had to have heating on.

She said, "And Palmer, did you think I owed you?"

"What? No..." He felt as if he was about to throw up. Put it down to the heat and the smell of new paint.

Bree-Anna said, "What I really wanted, an' you know because I told you, was a ring, not a necklace, an' a new flat, not a paint job!"

"You wanted more than I could give."

She didn't deny it. Left Palmer to back away and sit heavily at the kitchen table, dragging the back of his hand across his forehead.

"Did your wife cry?" Saying it, Bree-Anna looked as if she hadn't slept in days.

He was glad. "What kind of question's that?"

"If she had, you'd have blamed me!"

Palmer blamed her anyway. Considered upending the table and smashing the chair he sat on then using what was left of it to gouge holes in the walls but didn't. Just stood, turned, started to walk away.

When she told him he wasn't And Palmer and that she was Anna not Bree-Anna and that Allenby wasn't who he said he was, Palmer stumbled. Watching him as if he were an insect she'd plucked a leg from Bree-Anna said, "It would've been funny if you fell."

His mouth tasting of ash, he turned to face her. "Did he even go to Sandhurst?"

When Anna grinned at him Palmer's insides clenched as if he was plummeting from a great height. Why the fuck hadn't he seen this coming? Still grinning she said, "I'd ask you to give back my key, but I didn't ever give you one," turned away from him and ran water into the stained coffee cup.

Had whoever the fuck Allenby really was told Anna not to give him a key? Palmer didn't know where the thought had come from, but there it was, bright and hard-edged, impossible to blink away or step around.

A car sped along Cakemore Road, spearing him with its headlights. How did he look to the driver? Was his *Ted Baker* well and truly wrecked or did it just feel that way? He told himself it didn't matter and with difficulty made himself breathe slowly and deeply. He should climb down onto Cakemore Road and limp over to the 4X4. After what he'd done to it, it might be necessary for him to flag down a passing car. "Alright," he said. Back at his new flat would sleep and when he woke would finally unpack the *Dickins & Jones* suitcases and begin work. He could do it, was fucking sure that he could, when Palmer Developments was up and running would get a place with a real view of trees, fishing boats and stucco cottages, a dozen Armani suits, Ron Hill sportswear and a personal trainer. If he got lonely, he'd call the flapper and hear her tell him again that he looked like Leonardo Di-fucking-Caprio. He could get a Saab 900, but why the fuck would he when they'd gone bust? He'd find something else that really appealed and get whatever that was, only...

"*...Lauren...*"

His heart thrashing madly, Palmer turned left and right.

But it was him who'd whispered her name and lowered himself back onto the wasteland and scanned the shimmering darkness.

The motorway resumed its love song as Palmer's eyes settled on the outline of the building.

Still there was no sign of the old man. No matter, Palmer told himself. He'd find him and when he did, he'd take back the photo. Make it his. Nodded as, edging stealthily forwards, the night closed around him.

Biographies

Photograph by Gary Corbett

Wayne Dean-Richards has worked as an industrial cleaner, a fitness instructor, a painter and decorator and an actor. Currently he works as a teacher. Over a hundred stories have appeared in magazines and anthologies including *Birmingham Noir* and *The Cry of the Poor*. The Arts Council funded a collection of his stories: *At the Edge*—and a novel: *Breakpoints. Cuts*—a second collection of stories—is available from Amazon as an eBook, as is a collection of stories with his youngest son: *A Box of Porn*.

Tony Chenery currently works around the world as a surveyor of whales and dolphins. Formerly he has worked as a performance artist and as an Art Psychotherapist in the NHS. When at home he is most likely to be holed up in his studio painting.

Paul McDonald taught at the University of Wolverhampton for twenty five years, where he ran the Creative Writing Programme. He took early retirement in 2019 to write full time, and is the author of 20 books to date, the most recent being *Don't Use the Phone: What Poet's Can Learn from Books* (2023).